# SCOOPED

## A V-CARD DIARIES SPIN-OFF NOVEL

## LILI VALENTE

## SYLVIA PIERCE

# SCOOPED

*A V-Card Diaries Spin-Off Novel*

By Lili Valente and
Sylvia Pierce

# ABOUT THE BOOK

**In the market for a hot tip? Here's one: Don't bang your best friend's little sister.**

Especially when she's an investigative journalist and your investment company is the target of her latest scoop.

**Unfortunately, I have a thing for high-risk bets, and Ellie's suggestion that we mix business with pleasure is too sweet a deal to pass up.** Friends with benefits is the kind of low stress romantic situation a busy New Yorker actually has time for.

But it's not long before I'm falling harder than the post-bubble Nasdaq, hooked on Ellie's laugh and determination to make the world a better place.

There's only one problem...

**When it comes to risking money, I've mastered
every trick in the book.**

**But how the hell do I risk my heart?**

*Previously published as Falling for the Boss. Same fun, steamy
story, new cover and title!*

# PROLOGUE

Jack

They say money can't buy happiness, and that's probably true. But if your lot in life is to be a miserable prick, wouldn't you rather be a rich miserable prick?

Notice I didn't say a *selfish* prick.

Quite the contrary, ladies. I'm a generous man. My portfolio is *massive*, and I have the kind of hard assets guaranteed to deliver mutually pleasurable returns every time.

But mutual pleasure is where our arrangement ends. I learned long ago that unlike my bank account, love is *not* FDIC insured. So once my generous supply has met your eager demand, I'll be returning to the welcoming arms of my one sure thing—business, baby.

And it's booming.

My company is poised to become the go-to investment firm for elite athletes and entrepreneurs around the world. I have a penthouse apartment with a killer view of downtown Manhattan, a private office suite on the fifty-eighth floor, a vacation home in the south of France, and a net worth that just won't quit.

And you know what? I deserve it.

Think I'm cocky? Sorry to disappoint, but it's just numbers. Money is math and math is money—clearly defined rules, time-tested formulas, predictable answers —and that's about as un-cocky as it gets.

No, I wouldn't call it happiness, exactly...

But I've made my peace with it.

Hell, I've embraced it.

No complications, no emotions, and best of all—no losses I can't recoup.

And then *she* sweeps back into my life, and suddenly I'm not sure of anything anymore.

Except that I don't want her to go...

# CHAPTER ONE

## Eleanor

*A woman about to put her tube socks
and spirit glue where her mouth is...*

Day 1 Wednesday 8/1

"*I*t's like how colonel is pronounced KER-nal." Stephen draws out the last two syllables for the benefit of my tiny female mind. "Even though there isn't an 'R' in there."

I blink, stunned.

This guy can't possibly be for real. Can he?

It's hard to believe that just a week ago, I was thrilled at the prospect of spending time in a normal work environment. One where people don't sit at their desk in wrinkled pajamas with bed head, surrounded by coffee cups they haven't gotten around to washing even though their kitchen is literally three feet from their workstation.

I have good housekeeping intentions, I really do, but it's hard to care about a mess when there's never anyone around to see it. It's like the tree in the forest. If a mug —or a freelance journalist—goes unwashed in the privacy of her tiny Queens apartment, does she make a smell? I think not.

"You get it?" Stephen continues with a patronizing squeeze of my upper arm.

I nod, my lips pressed together to keep from saying something I shouldn't.

This is my brother's investment company—he and his partner Jack built it from the ground up. And Stephen is apparently a valuable member of their brokerage team, no matter how hard it is for me to imagine this douchebag closing a financial deal with anyone, let alone a famous athlete accustomed to a certain amount of deference.

"So Seyfried is like that." Stephen lifts his hands into the air, fingers spread wide in a ta-da motion. "You pronounce the 'G' before the 'F' even though it's not there. Because Seyfried and Siegfried are actually the same name if you look at it from an etymological standpoint."

I shake my head, dumbfounded. "Wow."

He grins. "Blew your mind a little, didn't I, slugger? Bam!" He reaches for my chin, but I duck, avoiding further fondling by drawing my cell from my purse.

"You did, Stephen. You really did." I glance out across the open plan office, praying I'll see Ryan's head bobbing above the crowd of people packing up for the day.

I'm not sure how much more of this I can handle. If my brother doesn't show in the next two minutes, I'll make a run for it and text him to call me when his plane touches down in Portland.

I've suffered through my fair share of mansplaining, but this is the first time I've had a guy explain how I'm mispronouncing my own last name.

Yes.

My. Own. *Last. Name.*

I've been Eleanor Seyfried—pronounced SIGH-fred, *not* SIG-freed—for twenty-eight years. One would assume I know how to pronounce it. Unless one were Stephen, or one of the other Wall Street dude-bros who make Seyfried & Holt a challenging place to work for anyone without a Y chromosome.

I would bet a thousand dollars Stephen has never dared to tell my brother that he's mispronouncing the name etched in gold outside his door.

"Have you explained this to Ryan?" I blink innocently as I point toward his office.

"Nah." Stephen's lips pucker and his brows dip into a V. "Ryan knows. He's a shark, your brother. Never stops swimming. Always thinking." He snaps his fingers several times, the sharp *snick* making my teeth itch. "Synapses always firing."

I'm about to tell Stephen that I understand Ryan's nimble brain well, because I also scored high on my GMATs—one hundred points higher than my brother, in fact. But before I can speak, Ryan emerges from the executive lounge.

"Ryan! There you are." My arm surges into the air, fingers wiggling. "Glad I caught you. I need a word before you leave for the airport."

"Sure thing, but I've only got five, ten minutes, tops." Ryan's brown eyes flick from me to Stephen and back again, a distracted smile on his face. "Hey, Rictor, how's the Ian Fox account going? You seal the deal?"

"Not yet, but I'm close," Stephen says, his chest puffing up. "Should have him on the hook by the end of the month."

"All right, but let's keep in touch on this one. He's primed to hit a new level with his career now that he's signed with the Badgers," Ryan says, throwing the rest over his shoulder as he pops into his office. "I'm meeting with him in Portland. I want to be sure we're all on the same page about what Seyfried and Holt can offer him that other wealth management companies can't."

"Gotcha, chief," Stephen says before winking and adding in a voice for my ears only, "Gonna miss your pretty face around the office, slugger. Don't be a stranger, okay?" He backs away, pointing at my chest. "And send us a copy of your article, when you're finished. My mom loves that stuff. She takes all my press mentions to church to show her friends. It's super cute."

"Super cute," I echo with a queasy smile as I lunge after Ryan, shutting his office door behind me with a combination sigh-groan that makes my brother laugh.

"A week out of your writer cave that rough on you, sis?" He smiles at me from across his massive oak desk, where he's busily tucking folders into his briefcase. "You appear to have showered recently. I'm impressed. Surprised...but impressed."

"Very funny. Yes, I've been showering daily, but that's not the problem."

"Glad to hear it." He taps at his cell, attention fixed on the screen. "Just in case you need to look for a job outside your lair, showering is a good life skill to keep in your arsenal."

"Again. Hysterical. You should do stand-up in your spare time." I keep my tone light, though the reminder of the tenuous nature of my freelance writing gig compared to Ryan's high-salaried, big-bonus position isn't the most welcome at the moment. Especially considering I might have to cancel the "Not Your Mother's Wall Street" article I've been working on for the editor at Barrington Beat. If I do, the week I spent here investigating will have been a waste of time. "But I need the not-funny Ryan right now. Seriously. There's a problem."

He looks up, his smile fading. "Is Dad okay?"

"Dad's fine," I say, with a frustrated huff. "Which you would know if you called him every Sunday. You know he wants you to call, too. It's family check-in, not Ellie check-in."

"But he keeps me on the hook for hours, El, and you make sure I stay abreast of all the news that's fit to print," Ryan says, his golden boy grin coming out to play.

"Speaking of fit to print... I can't write the article, Ryan. At least not the way I pitched it. It's not going to work."

His brow furrows. "What? Why not?"

"Because this *is* still our mother's Wall Street, or more like our father's." I wave my hand toward the world on the other side of his door. "Different technology, different slang, but it's still the same ol' boys' club underneath."

"What?" He props his hands on his hips. "But you said it yourself—we have more women working for S and H than any other financial firm our size. We've stepped up our recruiting efforts for female candidates, revamped our family leave policies... We're almost at a fifty-fifty male to female ratio for new hires, El. What other firm can say that?"

"Yes, and that's all great. But most of the female hires are making less money for the same jobs, or they're starting from the bottom while the men—many of them with less experience—are going straight into management positions," I explain. I can't believe my detail-obsessed brother has managed to overlook these facts. "And a lot of the women are only part-time. They don't have benefits, job security, or—"

"That can't be right," Ryan says with a shake of his head. "Have you talked to our hiring manager? Blair's been doing an amazing job."

"Blair's very busy," I say diplomatically, not wanting to get Blair in hot water, despite that fact that she's been an uncooperative B-word all week.

Being unable to get one of the two women in management positions at S&H to answer my questions hasn't made my job any easier, but I don't want to make unnecessary waves.

"You should pin Blair down before you leave." Ryan taps two fingers on his desk. "I haven't heard a single complaint from the new people. We're running like a well-oiled machine."

I sigh. "People aren't going to risk their already

uncertain positions by complaining to the boss, Ryan, but I've definitely heard rumblings of discontent."

"Like what?"

"Nothing I'm ready to share," I hedge, "but enough that I can't in good conscience write an article about my brother's ground-breakingly-awesome-for-ladies workplace at this juncture. I need time to dig deeper."

"Then take it," Ryan says. "If we have parity issues, I want to know about it. That's not the kind of company I want to run, El. I hope you know that."

"Of course I do." A rush of warmth fills my chest. With his good looks, razor-sharp mind, and Chosen One energy, Ryan could have become another entitled jerk like so many of his Harvard friends.

But that isn't my brother. He's a good man with a great heart, which is one of the major reasons I needed to have this conversation with him before my research goes any further.

"But if I'm going to keep digging, I need to have something to show for it," I continue. "Eventually I have to deliver a piece to Barrington, positive or negative. Are you okay with that?"

To his credit, Ryan hesitates only a second before nodding. "But I think you'll come to see this in a different light. Jack and I are pro-diversity and pro-equality." His glance shifts to the door behind me. "Right, Jack?"

"Indeed." Jack's laid-back drawl rumbles through the room like a soothing roll of distant thunder as the door snicks shut behind him.

But, as always, the presence of Ryan's partner and best friend is anything but soothing. I don't know what it is about the man, but Jack Edward Holt brings out my awkward, twitchy introvert like no one else.

I spin on my heel with a nervous laugh and a jerky wave. "Hey, how's it going, Jack? Didn't hear you come in."

His lips curve in his signature smirk, the one that assures you he's always in on the joke. "Going good, Ellie. Get everything you needed for your article?"

"She needs more time," Ryan says, answering for me in a big brotherly fashion that nevertheless rubs me the wrong way after spending a week with the patronizing and/or oblivious men on his staff.

They aren't all bad guys, for sure, but most of them could use a course in not interrupting their female colleagues while they're speaking and keeping jokes appropriate for the workplace. There's also the matter of the exotic odor emanating from the men's locker room in the company gym.

But hey, one battle at a time...

"And someone at the top to make sure she gets access," Ryan continues. "Can you handle that for me, Jack? I'm in Portland for the rest of the month."

"I don't know, I have a lot going on," Jack says at the same time I blurt out, "Jesus, Ryan, I don't need a babysitter."

Jack and I turn, gazes bumping as I try not to let my aversion to Ryan's proposal show. For his part, Jack looks uncharacteristically surprised.

But then, having his company rebuffed is probably a rare event for Mr. Holt. With his artistically mussed sandy-brown hair, sleepy green eyes, and long, lean, I-hit-the-gym-like-most-New-Yorkers-hit-the-coffee-shop frame, Jack is even more stupidly handsome than my brother. If Ryan is the golden boy next door, Jack is the bad boy with a voice like whiskey and a "let's break the rules" glint in his eye.

According to my brother—and the media who flock his way whenever the financial markets are making waves—Jack is a top-notch investor with the instincts of a man with twice the experience. But I'll never forget the Jack who got me stoned for the first time when I was twenty and then teased me mercilessly for the next two hours as I vacillated between laughing at his moaning zombie impression and clutching his arm in skin-crawling paranoia, terrified that my father was going to come downstairs and catch me being less than perfect.

And we won't even go into how mortifying it was to eat an entire bag of Cheetos in front of a person who has probably never had orange fingertips in his life. Even in his early twenties, Jack was too classy for Cheetos.

"I know you don't need a babysitter," Ryan says. "But you do need someone to make sure people answer your questions. And I know you're busting your ass with broker interviews, Jack, but surely you can spare some time. If members of our team are unhappy, I'd rather know about it sooner than later."

"Unhappy?" Jack's brow furrows as his gaze shifts my way. "Who's unhappy?"

"That's not something I'm ready to discuss." I stand up straighter, tugging the bottom of my slightly-too-large red blouse down over the top of my a-bit-too-small pin-striped skirt, acutely aware of how dumpy I look compared to the custom-made suits in the room.

"This is coming out of left field, isn't it?" Jack's tone

isn't unkind, but I'm losing patience, and I have two minutes left to convince Ryan to let me do this my way —sans babysitter.

"No, it's not coming out of left field," I say. "It's coming from the pitcher's mound, straight at your head. You know why Stephen calls me slugger? Because I asked why there are no women in the office fantasy baseball league and he told me none of them were interested. And I said, 'have you asked them?' And he just laughed and said, 'easy there, slugger,' and the name stuck."

Jack rolls a shoulder in something too elegant to be called a shrug. "Well, Rictor's a dick. Everyone knows that."

Ryan chuckles in agreement, making my blood pressure spike.

"It's not about one random dick," I say, my voice rising. "It's about the very real fucking differences in the way men experience this office culture versus the women."

Jack's eyes narrow thoughtfully on my mouth. "I've never heard you curse before."

"Well, I curse sometimes." My lips prickle, a buzzing sensation that intensifies the longer Jack stares. "When I'm passionate about something."

"Passionate is good," Jack says in his whiskey voice. "I respect passion."

"Good. That's g-good," I stammer, feeling twenty years old with Cheetos fingers again.

How does this man always manage to throw me off with no more than a word? A look? A blink of those snakeskin-green eyes that makes me feel like butterflies are dancing in my stomach?

Of course, I *know* why. It's because he's ridiculously sexy and I'm a lair-dwelling, loner writer weirdo who doesn't spend enough time around attractive men—or any men who aren't my neighbors or blood relatives, for that matter.

Jack would be so much easier to handle if I'd been that second son my father wanted.

But that's the story of my life. If only I'd been a boy, Mom dying when I was a toddler and me being raised in a bachelor's house—and everything that came after— would have been so much easier.

For everyone.

If only I'd been a boy...

An idea leaps suddenly into my brain, fully formed, like Athena ready to burst from Zeus's forehead.

But unlike Athena, my idea doesn't arrive draped in a Grecian tunic or carrying a brass shield. My idea is dressed in a three-piece suit and sporting a pair of swanky Italian leather dress shoes.

"So, it's settled?" Ryan shoots Jack a look that leaves no room for argument.

"Sure," Jack says, his gaze sliding my way. "We'll start tomorrow, Ellie?"

I look up, so excited by my shiny new idea that I can't help the giddy smile that spreads across my face. "Perfect."

*Oh, yes. We'll start tomorrow, Jack. And you won't know what hit you.*

## CHAPTER TWO
### Jack

*A man about to experience some **highly** unexpected new feelings for a co-worker's moustache…*

Day 2 Thursday 8/2

ow is it that we've invented phones advanced enough to stream movies and order groceries with a single tap, but no one can sort out how to make the subway smell less like urine?

Will scientists colonize Mars in my lifetime?

Will subways on Mars still smell like pee?

If people eat asparagus on Mars and pee on the subway, will the subway smell like pee, or asparagus?

These are the mysteries I ponder as I stare across my

mahogany desk, wondering if the guy I'm interviewing has any clue I've already voted him off the island.

"In conclusion," Brian says, "by utilizing Six Sigma strategies, I was able to radically streamline our core business process, eradicating inefficiencies in our product development lifecycle and increasing revenues by nine percent."

Nope. Not a clue.

"Impressive," I say. "So, you're a Six Sigma guy?"

"There's no problem it can't solve, and as a broker for Seyfried and Holt, I assure you, problem-solving would become my middle name."

"What's your middle name now?" I ask. Dick move, perhaps, but this is the seventh interview of the day, and each candidate has been as unimaginative as the one before. Blair was supposed to clear these guys in round one, sending me the cream of the crop.

But apparently she's looking for docile and predictable, a guy who will toe the company line.

Me? I prefer a little fire.

"Forgive me. Terrible sense of humor," I say, dialing it down. It's not this poor guy's fault I'm being blown off for lunch. No. That honor belongs to one Eleanor Seyfried, who hasn't bothered to return a single one of my texts.

Ellie Seyfried—now *there's* a problem Six Sigma can't solve.

"Tell me more about your client acquisition philosophy," I add.

I try to pay attention to Brian's answer. Honestly, I do.

But this thing with Ellie has me on edge, which is

definitely *not* my standard operating procedure. Sure, she's always thrown me off my game—even when Ryan and I were in grad school and she was still an adorably awkward college kid. But back then, I only saw her for occasional Seyfried family parties. And yeah, maybe I had a little crush, and enjoyed making her laugh way too much, but I thought I'd left all that behind.

Until now.

Having her in the office all week has seriously messed with my head.

Both of them.

If Ellie had any idea the kind of thoughts she stirs up —the kind of dreams that send me bolting for a cold shower at three in the morning, desperate for something to alleviate the ache and scrub my thoughts clean—my ass would've been hauled down to HR before the opening bell chimed on the stock exchange. And then she'd have her story gift wrapped with a bow, courtesy of my definitely-not-workplace-appropriate hard-on problem.

Fucking ironic, is what it is.

"...but that's all thanks to my contacts in the energy and biotech industries."

I drag my attention back to Brian, who's supremely pleased with himself. Just like the last guy. And the woman before him. The latest crop of MBA grads isn't lacking in confidence, that's for sure.

I let him natter on a bit longer, then wrap it up with a few noncommittal comments about next steps before I usher him out the door.

When my phone pings with a text a minute later, I

know I should be embarrassed at how fast I whip it out of my pocket, but I don't have time for that.

Shit. It's not Ellie.

It's her fucking big brother, like an omen from the universe warning me to cool it.

*Just locked in the Ian Fox meeting. Dinner tomorrow night.*

*Great,* I text back. *I'll let Rictor know.*

*How are the interviews panning out? Anything promising?* he asks.

*No stand-outs. Setting up a few more next week.*

*All right, keep me posted. Ellie giving you a hard time?*

If he only knew.

*Nothing I can't handle,* I text, then toss the phone onto my desk.

I'm trying to decide what the hell to do for lunch now that Ellie's off the menu, when in walks my assistant, Hannah.

"Eric Webb here to see you?"

"Webb?" I flip through the candidate file on my desk. Nothing for Webb. "I thought we were done for today."

"Apparently this guy is a friend of Ryan's. He says Ryan promised we'd squeeze him in?" Hannah scrunches up her face, her classic *WTF* look. "I'm guessing this is the first you're hearing about it, too. And I'm also guessing you haven't eaten anything since that disgusting kale smoothie this morning."

"Yep. And nope." Figures. Ryan's been so focused on the Portland office, it doesn't surprise me he forgot to mention the additional interview.

"Want me to blow him off and order your lunch?" she asks.

"No, that's not necessary. Send him in." Can't be

worse than Brian "Six Sigma" Andover, and lunch can wait.

Gives me an excuse to wait a little longer for Ellie, too.

*Pathetic, Holt. You need to get laid, and soon, before you make a fool of yourself.*

The new guy steps through the door, attaché case in hand, his smile guarded. He looks nervous—a touch gawky, too—wearing a suit that's a size too big and a mustache straight out of a 1970s porno.

"You'll have to forgive me." I move the folder in front of me to the side. "Ryan didn't have a chance to send over your resume, Mr.—Webber, was it?"

"Webb." His voice cracks, but he clears his throat and tries again. "Eric Webb."

"Eric Webb." I stand up to shake the guy's hand, which is slim and surprisingly soft—definitely not into pumping iron, this one. "How do you know Ryan?"

"At the risk of sounding cliché, he's a friend of the family," Webb says as we take our seats. "Our fathers went to Yale together. Frank was best man at my parents' wedding."

I nod, relaxing into my chair. Ryan's dad Frank is a hard-ass, but he's a good man, and definitely knows the business. If this guy is connected to Frank, he's gotta be good people.

"So. Why should I hire you, Eric?" I give him the fastball, no time for chit-chat. Guy doesn't miss a beat, though, fielding my questions with an ease his slightly unpolished appearance belies.

"You need me," he says matter-of-factly, "to diversify your strategic value proposition. You're getting great returns for your clients, generating lots of buzz on the street. But at the end of the day, you're still following the same old playbook."

I cross my arms and raise a brow. "Go on."

"I specialize in attracting and retaining risk-tolerant, high-net-worth clients looking for unconventional strategies in a time of market volatility and global instability. I've got a nose for emerging tech—we're talking *right* on the bleeding edge. Things most people never even hear about outside of science fiction."

Webb has me on the hook now. S&H deals mostly with athletes and celebs—people with lots of cash to play with—and they're always hot for the next big thing. And my friend, and client, Sam, the head of one of the world's most ground-breaking tech companies, is always telling me I need a tech nerd with vision in my corner.

If Webb can deliver that, I want him on my team.

I ask him a few questions about his experience, letting him wax poetic about his ideal portfolio mix. He has good instincts, the right blend of education and experience, and he knows his stuff.

But what I really need is a candidate who can think outside the MBA box and carry on a conversation about something other than ROI, APR, SEC, and the rest of the alphabet soup my analysts are swimming in.

I need someone who can charm clients and close deals.

I need someone creative, driven, and passionate.

I need someone who can take my mind off my best friend's little sister.

"What are you passionate about, Mr. Webb?" I interrupt a story about one of his former clients, surprising us both.

He waits a beat. Two. It's the first time he hasn't had a ready answer.

"P-Passionate?" he stammers.

"Yeah, something that lights you up inside, gets your juices flowing."

"Well, as I said, wealth management is—"

"Forget all that." I dismiss his comment with a wave. "I want to hear about the *real* you. Personally. Where do you spend your free time?"

"Personally?" He readjusts his tie, clearing his throat. "Well, I... I like the library."

Now we're getting somewhere. "A big reader, huh?"

At this, the guy lights up, a grin breaking his all-business demeanor. "If having my library card number memorized makes me a big reader, then yes." His mustache twitches with excitement, his eyes sparking.

I can't put my finger on it, but there's something about this guy... It's almost like we've met before. Maybe at one of Ryan's family gatherings? He said their fathers were friends. Could that be it?

"Tell me the last thing you read for fun," I say, hoping to catch another glimpse of that spark.

"Dragon Spell." He says it like he's daring me to laugh. When I don't, he continues, "It's about a wizard trying to resurrect a race of dragons, but he's the only person who believes they exist."

Webb goes on about the story, getting more amped up with every plot point. By the time he says, "...and then he discovers he's descended from dragon shifters," he's practically out of his chair with excitement.

In that moment, I know *exactly* why I recognize the spark in his eyes.

Because they aren't *his* eyes.

They aren't *his* anything.

Colored contacts, fake mustache, wig, the too-big suit and shoes...

Christ, I can't believe I didn't pick up on it sooner, but now that I have, it takes every ounce of willpower to keep my expression neutral.

Because the candidate sitting across from me gushing about dragons? Is none other than Ellie Seyfried in drag.

Do they still call it drag if it's a woman dressed as a man? I have no clue, but I know with absolute certainty that I've just been played. Hard.

Taking a steadying breath, I force a smile. "Tell you what, Mr. Webb. I've seen enough to know you're exactly the kind of candidate we're looking for."

"Really?" He—*she*, damn it—beams. "That's great."

"I'm ready to skip the rest of the hoop-jumping and call your references. Is there someone specific I can contact at—who was your previous employer? Hannaford Capital?"

"I... Sure. Of course." She makes a show of digging through her attaché case before clearing her throat. "To be honest, Mr. Holt, I wasn't prepared for things to move this quickly. Why don't I email you the information? Will that work?"

I steeple my fingers, staring at her over the tips. I don't blink. I don't look away. I don't even breathe.

To her credit, neither does Ellie, though I can feel the nervous tension rolling off her in waves.

I can't take another minute of it.

"Game over, Ms. Seyfried."

At this, Ellie scrunches up her nose and laughs. She actually *laughs*.

Jesus, this woman... I don't know whether to throttle her or kiss her.

"So you find this amusing? This...whatever it is you're doing?" I gesture from her shiny black loafers to the slightly-too-big suit coat draped over her shoulders, doing my best not to imagine the curves beneath.

"This," she says with a flourish, pushing out her chest in a way that's anything *but* masculine, "is my master plan. Say hello to your newest broker."

"You're not a broker."

"I am for the next few weeks, while I get the deep dive for my story."

I shake my head. "It will never work. No one's going to buy it."

"*You* bought it." Ellie's out of her chair now, pacing my office. "You just hired me!"

"And now I'm firing you."

"I can talk the talk, Jack. That's all that matters."

"It's not all that matters." I stand, circling around my desk and stepping into her path. "Do you feel even remotely guilty about trying to con your way onto my team? Is Ryan in on this?"

"No, and he doesn't need to be. This is *my* story, and I'm willing to do whatever it takes for authentic research." She lifts her stubborn chin, not wavering for a moment. "Gender inequality in the workplace is a huge issue. And as progressive as S and H is, you and my brother are still operating under the misguided assumption that an organic snack machine and free tampons in the bathroom are all it takes to create a supportive work environment... and..." Her nose wrinkles, and her breath rushes out. "What are you staring at?"

"Your, ah..." I swirl my finger in the general area of her mouth, where a strip of brown fuzz dangles precariously from her upper lip. "Your porn 'stache is falling off."

"Did you hear a word I said?" Clearly flustered, Ellie tries to push the thing back onto her face, inadvertently tearing off the other half. "And it's not a porn 'stache. It's —shoot. I had a feeling this would give me trouble."

"It was too close to your lip. Hold still." I cup her chin, tilting her face toward the light. Beneath her drawn-on man-brows, thanks to colored contacts, her normally blue eyes are dark brown. But they're still Ellie's, still swimming with hidden depths and a vulnerability that sends my heart jackhammering.

Without the mustache, her lips are full and soft, practically begging to be kissed, and it's all I can do not to devour her right here.

Forcing myself back to the task at hand, I press the mustache into place beneath her nose, my thumb brushing the corners of her mouth. Her skin is silky smooth, her upper lip glistening with a sheen of sweat that has me wondering what the rest of her body looks like when it's glistening, bare and glowing after I've brought her to the edge...

*Fuck.* This is bad. Real bad.

I should back off, put some distance between us before I do something incredibly stupid, but I can't seem to stop touching her. Can't pull my fingers away from the velvet heat of her skin...

*Get it together, asshole.*

"All set," I manage, forcing myself to return to my chair and silently count backward from ten.

"Thank you." She pats a finger across her lip from left to right, pressing the mustache in place. "This was kind of last-minute. More of a prototype disguise, really. I just need clothes that fit, some better glue, and—"

"No. You need a better idea. Ryan will never go for it."

"I can pull this off, Jack. It's the best way to get what I need. I've experienced the culture here as a woman—now I need to do it as a man."

"But you're *not* a man," I say.

And God, don't I know it. Crossing paths every day in the office last week was hard enough. Touching her? Staring at her mouth? Wondering what it would be like to taste those soft, lush, *entirely* female lips?

Yeah, I'm totally fucked.

"Please, Jack." She settles back into the chair across from me, fingers interlaced in her lap. "It's not like you're Mr. Rulebook. Ryan doesn't even have to know."

*Please, Jack? Don't tell Ryan...*

The words echo in my memory, and I fake a cough to hide my chuckle.

Had to be, what, eight years ago? Harvard winter break. I tagged along with Ryan for the holidays, crashing on the couch in their old man's basement. Night after Christmas, I'd just lit up a joint I'd been saving when I heard footsteps on the stairs.

I tried to play it cool, but Ellie knew right away what

I was up to. She flopped down on the couch next to me and nudged my knee with her snowman slipper. "Can I try?"

"Yeah, I don't think so," I said. "You're not even old enough to drink."

"If you're drinking that stuff, you're doing it wrong." She held out her hand and wriggled her eyebrows in that goofily cute way she had. "'Tis the season for sharing, Jack Holt."

Wordlessly, I caved, mesmerized by the curve of her lips as they encircled the joint. She sucked hard, making the end crackle and glow.

Then she turned green.

She coughed up half a lung, and I figured out pretty quick she'd never smoked before. Didn't deter Ellie, though. We shared the rest of it, watched some old Romero zombie flicks, and planned an apocalypse survival strategy with the kind of excruciating detail only the stoned can appreciate.

Then she went all in on a bag of Cheetos, freaked out about her father coming downstairs, and passed out on the couch. I spent the wee hours of the morning on the floor, shivering my ass off in a pair of shorts and a black Henley covered in her bright orange fingerprints.

I never told her this, but it was the best Christmas I'd had since I was a kid.

I wonder if she remembers...

"I'm going through with this," she says now, the softness vanishing from her eyes. "To borrow a phrase from the esteemed Rictor, I need to 'grow a pair.' So, you can help me, or you can stay out of the way while I grow my own, but either way it's happening."

Great. This isn't going away.

A laugh escapes my lips, and we both know she's got me by the balls.

But hell if I'm giving in without busting hers, first.

"In all your scheming, Eleanor, there's one problem you haven't considered." I pin her with the stone-cold gaze I reserve for special occasions, like getting a tight-ass client to part with his money.

She wavers, the space between her man-brows wrinkling. "What's that?"

I blow out a breath. "You're not going to like it."

"Tell me."

"It's bad. Probably a deal-breaker for you."

"Jack, will you just—"

"Our snack machine..." I deliver my final words in a whisper. "It's an organic, Cheetos-free zone."

Her gasp says it all.

*Oh yeah. She remembers.*

Her cheeks turn pink, and beneath that hideous mustache, her mouth rounds into an "o," sending a bolt of desire straight below the belt.

Hell. Every time I think I have the upper hand here, she undoes me all over again.

There's no way this arrangement can end well.

"That's fine," she says, regaining her composure. "I can bring my own." She rises from the chair and collects her case. "Does this mean you're in?"

I waver.

As much as I want to offer the support her inner fire deserves, I can't help my best friend's little sister infiltrate our company as a dude.

Not without putting myself in a precarious position

with Ryan, a guy who's been a damn loyal friend and the only real constant in my life. Not without violating some ethical standards and probably breaking a few SEC rules.

And definitely not without rocking a constant, raging, *highly* unprofessional hard-on. It doesn't matter what she's wearing—Ellie is still Ellie, and my cock knows it.

But damn it, I can already feel myself giving in.

"Well?" she demands.

I may not agree with her methods, but if Ellie needs my help, she's got it.

I meet her gaze across the desk and silence the warning bells clanging in my skull.

"Welcome aboard, Eric Webb. You and your porn 'stache start tomorrow, nine a.m. sharp."

# CHAPTER 3

Day 2 Thursday 8/2

ELLIE: Hey, are there stalls in the men's bathroom? If not, "Eric" might have to take breaks to run down to the coffee shop on the corner.

JACK: Probably? I have my own bathroom. Executive privilege, you know. You could always check with your buddy, Rictor.
P.S. Are you seriously texting me about pee breaks right now?
When this is over, you're going to OWE me. BIGLY.

ELLIE: Some of us have small bladders, Holt. And this is a key part of the Preparation for Possible Obstacles Phase of any journalistic mission.
P.S. Rictor is not my buddy. And you're going to owe ME bigly after I've added valuable perspective to your worldview.

P.P.S. I may or may not be peeing as I text this.

JACK: Too much information, Seyfried.

ELLIE: You're the one who wanted to be kept in the loop on every aspect of my probe. Just holding up my end of the bargain.

JACK: I appreciate your integrity, and I'm sure we'll find a way to accommodate your small bladder. You should be more worried about having the man cred to walk into the men's room in the first place.
It's not too late to back out.

ELLIE: I refuse to back out before I've even begun. Stop freaking out. I've got this, Jack. I promise.

JACK: Right... If you have any more burning bathroom questions, feel free to text me. I'll be up wondering what the hell I've gotten myself into.

ELLIE: Will do. Night, night, worrywart.

JACK: Good night, Eleanor. May you sleep well and have manly dreams.

ELLIE: You, too, boss man. ;-)

JACK: Oh, and Ellie? Be careful tomorrow, okay? For both our sakes.

# CHAPTER 4

## Ellie

Day 3 Friday 8/3

*B*e careful what you wish for, because you just might get it.

It's one of my father's favorite sayings, one I heard over and over again growing up. Like the time I begged for a pixie haircut (disaster). Or when I fought for a place on the track team then decided I hated running, jumping over hurdles, and just about everything track-flavored except hanging out with my friends on the way to the meets.

And then there was the Harvard Business School disaster, landing that coveted spot only to realize finance and I went together like peas and caramel corn.

Dad refused to let me quit track, and my regret didn't magically restore the twenty inches of hair I'd hacked off, but I did transfer from the business school to the journalism program halfway through my first year of grad school. I wasn't raised to be a quitter, but I can pivot when I need to.

Like when my sanity depends on it.

I could pivot right now, stay hidden at the back of the elevator, and ride it back down to the first floor where my roadkill-scented mustache and I can exit onto Vesey Street and disappear into the suited throng swarming the financial sector in search of coffee, bagels, and a place to smoke a pre-work cigarette.

No one would know I chickened out.

Well, no one except Jack, and he thinks I'm ridiculous anyway, so no journalist street cred lost there.

But I'm not ridiculous—I'm taking risks to get a unique angle on this story—and I'm not going to let fear win.

I've got this. I'm wearing a new suit that fits where it should and sits low enough on my hips to hide my curves. My wig is Broadway quality, borrowed from the best costume-designing neighbor in the world, who also agreed to part with his second-best fake mustache—as opposed to the fourth-best 'stache I wore yesterday.

Having a neighbor who has a collection of fake mustaches—and the skill with cosmetics to teach me how to work masculine magic on my face—is a sign that my plan is destined to succeed. Jack only saw through my disguise because he's known me for years and yesterday's attempt was admittedly half-assed.

But today, I'm ready.

I'm a testosterone-fueled man-beast ready to take my new office by storm! Grr!

Rolling my shoulders back, I suck in as deep a breath

as possible with two elastic bandages squishing my breasts into pancakes, ignore the dead-animal stink of the super-powerful spirit gum holding my smaller, less porn-tastic mustache in place, and step out into the S&H reception area.

But after getting up an hour early to put on my man face, all I can think about now is an extra-large cup of coffee.

The underling break room is a simpler affair than the executive lounge where my brother and the higher ups recharge, but still far swankier than any water-cooler situation I encountered in my years of working in a newsroom. There is a full kitchen, two stainless steel refrigerators, the Cheetos-less organic snack machine, a variety of seating options, and a gourmet coffee station that puts Starbucks to shame, complete with everything I need to make a caramel latte.

Now to find my way through the crowd swarming the machine and figure out how to work the milk frothing thingamajiggy...

"Hey, new guy." Hannah, Jack's assistant, a curvy, freckled redhead with kind brown eyes smiles as I sidle up to the coffee queue. "Eric, right?"

I nod, dropping my pitch as low as I can manage. "Yeah. Nice to see you again, Hannah."

Her brows bob in surprise. "You, too. You're good with names, I see."

"I try to be." I smile my new, careful smile. Men, especially financial sector men, don't smile as widely as women, and caution is good for keeping the mustache in place.

"That'll serve you well, but don't be afraid to ask if

you forget someone. It's a big office, and we've all been the newbie." She laughs before gesturing toward the break room door. "And remember, I'm down the hall if you need anything. Jack asked me to keep an eye on you, make sure you get settled in okay."

"That was nice of him," I say, figuring now is as good a time as any to start putting out my undercover feelers. I asked around last week, but people weren't inclined to dish with the boss's sister. Now that I'm a peer, I'm hoping they'll be more loose-lipped. "Jack seems like a fun person to work for. I'm looking forward to being part of his team."

Hannah's smile widens. "He is fun. Fair, too, which isn't always a given."

Before I can ask what she means, a seal-bark of laughter sounds from the door. "No, *you* get the hell out," Rictor shouts, jabbing his thick finger at someone farther down the hall. "Yeah, I do kiss your mother with this mouth. Ask her." Still guffawing, Rictor swaggers into the room. "Hey there, Hannah Banana. Any almond milk in here? The lounge is out."

"Why don't you open the fridge and check, Stephen," she says, her lips tightening at the edges. "And meet Eric while you're at it. He's the new broker."

Rictor thrusts an arm into the air between us as his eyes sweep my frame. But his gaze is calculating, not speculating, giving me my first taste of the difference between being Ellie and being Eric.

Ellie had her boobs checked out and was complimented on her skirt. Eric gets a firm handshake and a, "Great to have you on board, man. What's your specialty?"

As I roll through my spiel about emerging technologies, Hannah backs toward the door with a wiggle of her fingers.

I stop mid-sentence to wave and say, "Thank you, Hannah. I appreciate the welcome."

"My pleasure," she says before stepping out into the hall and the salmon run of people hurrying to get to their desks before the stock exchange opens.

Rictor grunts out a laugh as he crosses to the fridge. "Don't even think about it, bro. She looks like a firecracker, but under all that ginger, she's cold as ice."

"Excuse me?" I turn to him with a frown.

"Getting in her pants," Rictor clarifies, his voice low. "It's a no-fly zone down there, I promise. Better men than you have tried."

My jaw drops. I can't believe he's taking the conversation *there* not thirty seconds after meeting me—and with six other employees, most of them women, standing less than four feet away at the coffee machine.

I'm still trying to figure out how "Eric" responds to stuff like this, when my butt begins to vibrate. "Barbie Girl" by Aqua blasts from the speakers, filling the break room with a sugary-pink pop song so girly I might as well rip off my pants and prove beyond a shadow of a doubt that I'm in possession of a vagina.

I struggle to pull my phone from my tiny back pocket, sweat breaking out beneath my fake 'stache. Finally, I wrestle my cell free and silence the pop-abomination amidst giggles from the women stirring creamer into their coffees a few feet away.

"Got a thing for Barbie, huh?" Rictor casts serious side-eye my direction.

"My neighbor's daughter must have done that last night," I say as I decline Spencer's call. I'm not ready to give him a breakdown on project Trojan Mustache just yet. "She borrows it to play Scrabble and then changes my ringtones to the most embarrassing things possible. It's part of a prank war she started when she was eight and decided a wo-working, um..." I clear my throat with a nervous laugh. "A working guy living alone needed a kid influence in his life."

Shoot, I almost said "woman living alone."

I almost blew it five freaking minutes into my first day!

"Prank war, huh?" Rictor grunts. "I think it's safe to say the kid won."

"Well, I think it's cute," a rosy-cheeked brunette I don't remember meeting last week pipes up from near the snack machine. "It's sweet that you're good with kids. Shows character."

"I don't know that I'm good with kids in general," I confess. "But Sonia's a good friend. Her other dad passed away a few years ago, and since then our whole floor has chipped in to help Spencer out. Being a single parent isn't easy anywhere, I'm sure, but it seems extra hard here in the city."

More murmurs of appreciation fill the air and one woman presses a hand to her heart as she announces, "That's it. I've got my new favorite broker. Anything you need, Eric, you let me know. I work support for Bruce Maddox and Kyle Hershman, but I can always fit you into my schedule."

Cheeks flushing with embarrassment, I thank her and excuse myself, fleeing the room without coffee while

Rictor glares at me with thinly disguised contempt for my less-than-manly display. Back at my desk, I settle in with headphones and the Seyfried & Holt orientation video queued up on my computer, determined to get back on track and stay under the radar.

I'm here to blend in, bear witness, and bring back observations from the front lines of the gender-inequality war, none of which is going to happen if I blow my cover on my first day.

Thankfully, the rest of the morning passes peaceably, and I spend my lunch hour in a booth at the back of a nearby Russian bistro, eating spine-strengthening red cabbage soup and steeling myself for another five hours of manliness.

But I probably should've eaten two orders. By the time the two o'clock meeting rolls around, I'm already drained.

I've underestimated how exhausting it would be to micromanage every move, every breath, every word and non-verbal response, from the way I laugh to the sound I make when I bang my knee—*hard*—on the metal leg of the conference table.

My high-pitched yip of agony goes mostly unnoticed in the chaos as people settle in for the meeting, but Jack's sharp green gaze shifts my way, his lips twisting with disapproval. I smile reflexively—my usual anxious, Jack's-in-my-vicinity grin—before I remember to be manly and take my grinning down a notch.

But the anxiety triggered by Jack's glare remains.

It's the first time I've seen him since our one-on-one time in his office yesterday, and for some reason I can't stop staring at his hands. At his fingers, to be precise, those strong, capable fingers that so gently pressed my mustache into place while Jack's body heat made my skin flush beneath my ill-fitting suit and Jack's unique scent bloomed in the air around me, a heady mix of eucalyptus, fennel, and a spicy, clean scent that makes my mouth water.

The man smells good enough to eat.

Or at least to lick.

To lick all over, up and down, until I've explored every inch of his tanned, toned, utterly delicious—

"I'd also like to welcome Eric Webb to the team," Jack says, motioning my way.

I flinch in my chair—*must* pay attention and stop thinking about licking my fake boss, who is *every bit* as off-limits as if he were my real boss, *if not more so*—and lift a hand, wiggling my fingers. "Thanks. Excited to be here."

"Excited to have you." Jack's frown belies the words of welcome. He's clearly not thrilled about his role in my sting operation, but I do my best to ignore his grumpiness and hope my coworkers will do the same.

I cross my legs and snatch a pen from the middle of the table, ready to take notes and contribute to the best of my ability. But focusing isn't easy when Jack keeps shooting judgmental, disapproving, and even one vaguely nauseated look in my direction, making me wonder if other people can smell my icky glue stink. I thought I was the only one suffering, because it's literally right under my nose, but maybe I was wrong.

Thankfully, Jack guides the meeting with a steady hand, and by the time three o'clock rolls around, he's sending everyone back to work with a "good job team, keep it up."

Snatching my notepad from the table—my loopy, flourish-filled cursive might be a lady-tell, now that I think about it—I leap to my feet and start for the door, only to hear Jack's deep voice call my fake name.

"Webb, meet me in my office in five."

I turn to face him, mortified by the pity that flashes across the faces of the two men easing around me to get to the door.

Why is he calling me out on my first day? Drawing attention to me when the best thing for my article is to draw as little focus as possible?

I'm about to ask him these exact questions—under my breath, of course—when he pauses in front of me and says in a husky whisper, "Your mustache is slipping. Again."

My fingers fly to my lip. I adjust it as best I can and mumble, "I'll put some more glue on in the bathroom."

"Do that, and then come to my office. Immediately. Do not pass go, do not flounce to the break room for coffee, do not—"

"Flounce?" I prop my hands on my hips with a huff. "I have never flounced a—"

"And hands off your hips," he murmurs. "I can see everything you're trying to hide, Eleanor."

My lips part and my hands drop to my sides as a wave of completely inappropriate heat washes through me.

Damn it, why does his voice have to be so motorcycle-idling-by-the-ocean sexy? It makes everything he says sound vaguely suggestive, and apparently vaguely is all it takes to make my skin tingle and my body ache.

"Everything's fine," I whisper. "No one suspects a thing."

His gaze drops to my mouth and lingers there long enough to make breathing difficult. "You now have two minutes," he finally says, breezing past me with a disinterested expression.

I spin, intending to tell him I don't appreciate the alpha-hole behavior, but several coworkers are still hovering near the exit. I swallow the retort and head for the bathroom, getting so close to the ladies' room that my hand is reaching for the door handle before I remember what kind of parts I'm supposed to have and dart across the hall to the mercifully empty men's room instead.

After locking myself in the only stall—thank God, sweet stall—I pull my compact and glue from my suit pocket and make the appropriate fixes to my stinktastic 'stache before tugging out my phone and shooting Spencer a text: *Even the super stinky super glue is failing me, Spence. Got anything else I can try to keep me from losing my facial hair in my next cup of coffee?*

*Oh no,* he texts back. *If it stinks, it's probably expired. I'll pick up some fresh on my way out of the shop after the show tonight. How's your debut going?! I've been on pins and needles all day!*

Stifling a groan, I reply, *Not awful, but not great. I'm about to get a dressing down from the boss man.*

*Don't let him grind you down, honey,* Spence texts. *I respect your commitment to your craft. Stay the course, and the boss man will, too.*

I type out a quick thanks, but Spencer's sweet words aren't as encouraging as they would usually be.

What if I don't have what it takes to pull this off? What if my acting skills and my journalistic skills are both subpar and this entire endeavor is destined to fail?

And almost as worrisome—what if this weird awareness of Jack as a delicious creature worthy of hours of devoted licking gets worse?

I've always been anxious around Jack and aware of him in a way I'm not with most men, but I've never wanted to straddle him in his desk chair and explore his stupidly sexy mouth with my tongue before. I mean, maybe I did...a little, but I could always ignore the forbidden voice of temptation.

"And you'll *keep* ignoring it," I whisper to my reflection in the compact. "Because he is off-limits, a cocky egomaniac, and most definitely not thinking of you as anything but a pain in his ass he would like to have surgically removed ASAP."

With a nod, I snick my compact closed and head for Jack's office, mustache *and* defenses firmly in place and fingers crossed that they'll stay that way.

# CHAPTER 5

## Jack

Day 3 Friday 8/3

"Close the door." I don't give Ellie a chance to sit before I start in on her. "You've got thirty seconds to convince me not to shut this whole thing down."

"What? Why?" She turns from the door and walks—sashays, rather—toward me, making me more aware of her curves with every swish of her hips, despite her low-riding men's dress pants. "We had a deal, Jack. You're supposed to back me up."

"And you're supposed to lay low, but clearly there's been a miscommunication about—"

"*Lie.*" Ellie sighs as she flops into the chair across from my desk.

"I beg to differ. We agreed—"

"No, I mean the phrase. It's *lie* low. Lay is the past

tense of lie, as in—I lay low yesterday, but today I'm going to lie low. Present-tense lay refers to something you physically do to an object."

Fucking hell.

I'd like to present-tense lay *her*, right here on my desk. And maybe in my fifteen-hundred-dollar ergonomically superior Herman Miller office chair.

I pinch the bridge of my nose and squeeze my eyes shut, forcing the entirely-too-detailed image out of my head before I do something insane, like ask Ellie if she's interested in a little afternoon delight. I have a meeting in ten minutes, and ten minutes isn't nearly enough time for a woman like Ellie. I'd want to savor every moment of her, the sweet taste of her kiss, the silky-smooth feel of her skin, the sounds she'd make as—

"Sorry for being the grammar police," she says, biting her lip. Her voice yanks me out of the fantasy, but the lip-nibbling does nothing to ease the ache below my belt. "That's what you get for hiring a writer."

"I'm well aware of what I signed up for with *you*, Eleanor." I say, taking pleasure in the way her eyes spark when I say her full name. I use her momentary distraction to adjust myself in my chair, grateful for the giant slab of a desk that's presently hiding my crotch. "My point remains. People are already asking questions."

"What people?"

"Rictor was in here twice. Wanted to know how well I vetted the new guy. He's not sure you fit the mold."

"The Rictor mold? *Please*. I can do Stephen 'Dude-bro' Rictor all day long." Ellie clears her throat and reclines in the chair, casually tossing one arm over the back. "Hey, bruh! You catch the game this weekend? Killer, am I right? Dude, you see the new waitress at Blue Bay? She's tight as hell. I'm totally gonna hit that. And seriously, I got the hookup on these biotech stocks, bruh. You in it to win it? No? Fine, but don't come crying to me when you're caught with your dick in the wind."

I raise an eyebrow, barely holding back a laugh.

She pins me with a narrow look. "You know I'm right."

"Twice in the span of five minutes," I tease. "Must be a new record."

This gets a grin, but it doesn't last long.

"I'm not walking away from this, Jack." Ellie's smile fades. "Not for Rictor or anyone else. It's a good story. And it's important."

"I understand. I wouldn't have agreed to this if I didn't believe it was important. But—"

"Seventeen." She crosses her arms over her chest, refusing to give an inch. "That's how many instances of overt sexism I've already witnessed today."

I lean forward, all traces of our earlier jokes gone. "I'm listening."

"Aside from the 'locker room' talk?" Ellie pulls a small steno pad from her inside coat pocket, flipping past several pages of notes. "We have men expecting high-level female colleagues to fetch their coffee, taking credit for women's work and ideas, and allowing clients to treat female brokers as if they're about as qualified as the potted plants in the break room."

"Really?" My gut clenches. S&H is supposed to be different. A fair, fun, and challenging place to work.

That's how Ryan and I always envisioned it—for *every* employee, regardless of salary or title.

How did we get so far out of the loop on this?

Looking around my posh office, I have my answer. I may as well be in a damn ivory tower. I'm insulated from the day-to-day here, from all but the senior staff. We don't even share the same break room.

"As far as I'm concerned—and I know Ryan feels the same way—none of that is acceptable," I say. "But generalizations and observations aren't enough. Not for your article, and not for HR to start making real changes." I gesture toward her notebook. "What else have you got?"

"You want hard data? Listen to this: not a single female broker makes an equivalent salary to her male counterparts here, even after adjusting the data to account for different experience levels and client loads."

I frown. "That...can't be right. That's not how our compensation package works. It's a merit-based system that rewards high performers with commissions and bonuses."

"What about the workers who are never given the chance to prove their merit? The ones who are passed over for the plum accounts, or given fewer opportunities for continuing education? And look at your hiring practices." Ellie glances back at her notes, dragging her slim finger down the page. "Four out of five management positions in the last two years have gone to men. A lot of well-qualified female candidates weren't even granted interviews."

I consider her words, embarrassed that I can't explain away any of this. "I had no idea. I mean, I should have. It just never occurred to me to check."

She shrugs. "Welcome to the seedy underbelly of the patriarchy."

"I don't—"

We're interrupted by a knock on the door, followed by Hannah peeking her head in. "Sorry for the intrusion, but you have a meeting in Conference B in five minutes."

"Thanks, Hannah. I'll be right there."

"Great." Hannah smiles. "I've prepped your notes—they're out here on my desk. Would you like a coffee or anything?"

I open my mouth to take her up on the offer, but a bolt of guilt lances my gut.

Is Hannah compensated fairly? Am I doing enough to ensure she has access to the same advancement opportunities as her male peers? Have I ever said or done anything to make her feel insignificant or undervalued?

"No thanks," I tell her. "I'm good. Oh, and Hannah? You're doing an excellent job. We should set up a time next week to talk about your goals."

"My...goals?" Hannah scrunches up her nose with a laugh. "As in, life goals? Dinner goals? Squad goals?"

"Just...put something on the calendar."

She nods, sobering as she realizes I'm serious. "Sure thing."

After she ducks out, I turn back to Ellie. "How did you find out about all of this?"

"S and H keeps records of applications and interviews, as well as salary data."

My eyes widen. "You hacked into the HR databases?"

"Me? A hacker?" Ellie scoffs. "Now, my friend

Gregory in college? That guy could hack his way into the NSA. I'm lucky if I can remember my bank card pin."

"So how do you know about the hiring data?"

She shrugs. "I made a few friends in a few strategic places."

I glance at my watch. "In the five hours you've been here?"

"This isn't amateur night, Jack," she says, sitting up straighter. "It's my job as a journalist to suss out the facts, and in case you and my brother—and my father, since we're naming names—haven't noticed, I'm good at it."

"I don't doubt your ability to get the scoop," I assure her as I rise from my chair to head out for my meeting.

"Then what's the issue?" She stands, too, folding her arms and cocking out a hip, proving my point.

She's intelligent, passionate, and completely capable.

But she's *not* a dude.

"Your cover is the issue," I say. "This assignment is going to take more digging than either of us anticipated. You'll be in this office every day for weeks—maybe longer. And each day is another opportunity for someone to figure out Eric isn't what he seems to be. If that happens, we're both screwed. And let's not even talk about what Ryan would do."

"I don't like keeping him in the dark any more than you do," Ellie says softly, placing a hand on my forearm. "But he's not here. We need to move on this. And I need to stay undercover."

"That's why we need to strategize. Maybe over dinner tonight?"

"I have a date tonight. But Saturday and Sunday are open."

"A date?" Jealousy flares inside my chest. It can't be a guy from the office—at least not one who knows her as Eric. Did someone on my staff ask her out last week, when she was still wearing skirts and earrings and that sweet, all-too-innocent smile? "Anyone I know?"

*Please don't be Rictor. Please don't be Rictor...*

"I'm not sure this conversation is workplace appropriate." Ellie smiles, lighting me up from the inside, despite the raging Jealousy Beast clawing through my gut. "Now, if you'll excuse me, I have work to do."

"So, you're free tomorrow morning, ten o'clock?"

Ellie narrows her eyes. "What are you plotting, Holt?"

"That's *Professor* Holt to you. Welcome to Dude 101," I say with a smile, finally regaining some of the control I've lost in the last day. Agreeing to her methods may have been a mistake, but I'm not going back on my word. We're partners in crime now, and I need to make damned sure she's got what it takes to pass as a man.

Not just once in a while, but every second she's posing as a card-carrying, dick-swinging member of S&H Investments.

"Class begins at ten a.m. at your place," I continue, enjoying having the upper hand. "I expect you to be prepared with your dude talk, your dude walk, and a boundless appetite for knowledge of the Y-chromosomal nature. *Intimate* knowledge."

Ellie's looking at me like I'm nuts, but she hasn't said no. And while there's a small voice inside me insisting that this Dude 101 bullshit is just an excuse to spend time with her outside of work, the fact remains that I can't let her go off half-cocked—rather, *no*-cocked—while I sit back and watch this blow up in our faces. There's too much at stake to leave it up to her good intentions and a questionable tube of mustache glue.

So while she's sifting through my company's dirty laundry, I'll be doing everything in my power to keep the swish out of her step, the sparkle out of her eyes, and that *highly* unmanly, fantasy-inducing pout off her pretty face. With any luck, we'll fix whatever's going on at S&H, she'll get a killer story, and I'll nip this ridiculous crush in the bud before I do something we'll *both* regret.

"Oh, and Miss Seyfried?" I open the door, gesturing for her to exit in front of me, flashing her a wolfish grin as she brushes past. "Insubordination will *not* be tolerated."

# CHAPTER 6

## Ellie

Day 4 Saturday 8/4

*B*y nine fifty the next morning, I have my Eric duds laid out on the sofa for inspection, tea and coffee on the kitchen table in case Dude 101 requires additional caffeine, and I'm slipping out of my apartment to fetch my new, extra-sticky mustache glue from Spence.

Dude lessons. *Seriously.*

I *do not* need dude lessons.

What does Jack think I've been doing for the past twenty-eight years? I grew up in a house full of men, I wore my brother's hand-me-downs until I was fourteen, and until my bad haircut grew out and my boobs grew in (sometime around tenth or eleventh grade), I was mistaken for a boy at least once a week.

I practically *am* a man. At least on the inside.

I certainly feel more comfortable with men than women.

Then again, karaoke with a few of the ladies from the office last night was a blast. I didn't score any information for my article—it was too loud in the back of the Korean restaurant—but it was so much fun. No one pressured "Eric" to sing, no one judged the people who did let out their inner diva—even when Barb from accounting massacred *My Heart Will Go On.* Twice. And I was home by a respectable ten-thirty.

I would be totally rested, in fact, if I hadn't tossed and turned until one in the morning, stressing about being alone with Jack in my tiny apartment.

Sexy, sanity-testing, lick-able, off-limits Jack.

Why my twisted libido has decided *now* is a good time to develop an even more serious crush on Jack than the one I had in college, I have no idea. Probably because it's a traitor, like my upper lip, which seems determined to de-sticky-fy every brand of mustache glue known to man.

"You should never have agreed to this," I grumble, though I know I had no choice. Jack made it clear when he dismissed me yesterday that "no" was not an option.

*I wonder if he's that much of a control freak in the bedroom...*

Ugh. Now is *not* the time for fantasizing about the sexual proclivities of my brother's best friend. I need to get my glue, get home, and get my game face on.

I'm knocking softly on Spence's door—hoping he and Sonia aren't sleeping in—when the elevator pings open behind me, and Jack steps out.

I'm not even facing his direction, but I *know* it's Jack

from the eucalyptus, spice, and sexy-as-sin man scent drifting down the hall.

Damn it, he's early!

I curse beneath my breath as Sonia opens the door, her dark, corkscrew curls forming a sleep-mussed halo around her face.

"My, my...a quarter for my swear jar so early in the morning?" Sonia's smile lights up her cherub's face, the one that belies the mischief-maker within. "Not like you, Ellie Bellie, but thank you for starting my morning off right."

"Yeah, yeah, I'll drop it off later." I glance over my shoulder to see Jack prowling our way, looking ridiculously stylish in gray slacks and a white button-down. I hold up a finger—indicating I'll be right with him—and turn back to Sonia. "I need to grab that glue your dad scored for me."

"Just a sec." Sonia takes a breath, clearly preparing to shout for her father instead of going to get him, in the way of nine-year-olds everywhere, when Spencer appears behind her.

"Heard you knock." He holds up the glue with one hand as he wraps an arm around Sonia's shoulders with the other. The contrast between Spencer's vampire-pallor—a hazard of working in dark theaters—and Sonia's golden-brown skin is even more startling today than usual.

But before I can ask him if he's sure that he's getting enough vitamin D, Spence spots Jack down the hall, and his blue eyes sparkle to life. "Oh, sweet baby Jesus," he murmurs. "Who is that?"

"Thank you." I take the glue. "That's my boss. And

my brother's oldest friend. And my friend. Sort of. Sometimes." I sigh. "It's complicated."

"Sounds like it." Spencer's blond brows wiggle. "So *that's* the boss man. How have we not heard more about this Tall Drink of Delicious Complications?"

"She's been holding out on us." Sonia nods, her lips puckering judgmentally.

"Don't be crazy." I back away, refusing to tell either of these lovable gossip hounds anything about Jack. "Catch you two later."

"Later, Ellie," they singsong in a way that makes my cheeks flush pink, ensuring I'm more flustered than usual by the time I reach where Jack is leaning against the wall by the fake potted fern.

"Aren't you going to introduce me to your friends?" he asks, his voice cool.

"They just woke up," I say, continuing down the hall. "And I figured you'd want to get right to work, correct? Since I'm so desperately in need of assistance?"

Jack crosses his arms, standing way too close as I work my key into my lock.

Damn it, why does he have to smell so good? And be so warm and magnetic and tingle-inducing?

"Interesting tone." He follows me inside, glancing around my much-cleaner-than-usual apartment with an arched brow. His eyes widen when he spots my bed against the far wall—hard to hide it when you live in a studio—but thankfully he doesn't comment. "You don't think you need help?"

"I don't." I toss the glue onto the coffee table beside my mustache and do-it-myself dude makeup. "I just needed fresh glue, and Spencer brought me some from his costume shop. So I'm all set."

Jack snorts. "Set to blow your cover before you even get started. If you hadn't spent half of yesterday watching orientation videos, you would've been made. The way you walk alone is—"

"So maybe my walk isn't super masculine," I cut in, propping my hands on my hips. "Not all men are, you know. There are plenty of guys in New York who have a little swing in their step."

"You don't walk like a man with a swing in his step," Jack says flatly. "You walk like someone who's never had a dick between your legs. There's a difference."

Heat floods to my face, but before I can think of an appropriate response to that bombshell, Jack waves a hand in the air between us.

"I didn't mean it like that..." He shakes his head, wincing as if the thought of me with a dick between my legs makes him queasy. "I meant, you walk like a woman who has woman parts, and eventually people are going to notice. Bare minimum, that needs to be addressed before Monday."

I cross my arms, wishing I'd changed out of my yoga pants and comfy tee into something that made me feel less scrubby and powerless. Ryan's right—clothes are more important than I give them credit for.

So maybe Jack is right, too...

No matter how much I would like to believe I didn't make an idiot of myself yesterday, Jack has the same sharp eye as my brother. And even if he's wrong, advice from someone who has been an *actual man* his entire life can't hurt. Besides, he has skin in this game, too. The least I can do is play along.

"Fine," I grumble, my shoulders hunching. "Teach me how to walk."

Jack exhales. "I'll try, but not while you look like that."

"Like what? Like I woke up half an hour ago? Sorry, but that's not my fault. That's *your* fault for inviting yourself over at a ridiculously early hour for a Saturday."

"I was thinking like a crab refusing to come out of her shell," Jack says, his tone cooling again. "But please accept my apologies for the early hour. I assume your hot date went well, then?"

I bite my lip, eyes lifting guiltily to the ceiling, wishing I hadn't let that fib out the door. "You could say that."

"So, who is he?" Jack moves closer, hands sliding into his pockets in that too-relaxed way that always makes me nervous.

"Why do you care?"

"I don't." He's so close now that I have to tilt my head back to maintain eye contact, a fact that has my pulse jumping. "But you're struggling to pull this off as it is, without some random guy keeping you out all night."

"It wasn't a guy," I confess. "I went out with Lulu, Paige, and a couple other girls from the office for Korean food and karaoke."

For a second Jack looks almost relieved, but then his forehead bunches again. "Tell me you didn't sing."

I roll my eyes hard. "I'm not a hundred percent solid on my man voice when I'm *talking.* I know better than to belt out Blaze of Glory."

His lips curve. "So, you admit it. You need my help."

"I need practice," I say, meeting him halfway.

"Then let's get to work, Seyfried." He points a finger at the couch. "Man clothes. Now. And this time stuff a sock in it."

I blink. "A sock in what? My mouth?"

"Not a bad idea, but I meant down your pants. Until you master the art of pretending you've got something down there, you should use a prop." He steps back, his gaze sweeping up and down my frame, inciting a sudden urge to fidget. "But nothing too big. No one's going to buy that Eric is packing heat."

I'm tempted to ask why not—surely you can't judge cock-size by a guy's build—but think better of it. Considering my tendency to blush when Jack's around, that doesn't seem like a wise line of questioning. The sooner I can ease his fears and get him out the door the better.

Ten minutes later, I emerge from the bathroom dressed in my Eric gear—minus the mustache, man wig, and makeup—to find Jack has helped himself to tea.

When he sees me he stops mid-sip, setting the mug back on my kitchen table. "Where's the sock?"

I shift from one foot to the other, trying to remember if I've ever felt more self-conscious than I do at this moment, with Jack's attention laser-focused on my crotch. "I didn't have a spare sock in the bathroom, so I improvised."

Jack arches a dubious brow, but thankfully doesn't question me. He does *not* need to know I have a shower cap wrapped in toilet paper nestled between my thighs.

Strategically avoiding the bed, he sits at the kitchen

table and motions to the only clear stretch of hardwood in my six hundred square foot studio—the pathway from the door to the kitchen table. "All right. Show me what you've got."

"Fine." Lifting my chin—*fake it till you make it!*—I cross to the door, turn, and execute my best dude walk. One foot in front of the other, shoulders back, no hip swaying, no bounce in my step.

Jack's expression remains eloquently unimpressed.

"What?" I reach the table and prop a hand on my waist. "What was wrong with that?"

"Where do I start?" He casts a pointed look at my hip. "And every time you stick one of those out you give yourself away."

"Well, I'm not trying now. I'm taking a break for feedback."

"No breaks for feedback." He snaps his fingers. "Stay in character, keep the curves hidden, remember you have a penis. Go. Again."

And so, I do it again.

And again.

And again, until I'm so self-conscious my eyelid is twitching, and walking starts to feel as unnatural as riding a bicycle under water.

"Now you look like a robot," Jack says.

"I feel like a robot," I huff in frustration. "This isn't working. You're making me nervous, and I stink at learning things when I'm nervous."

"Why am I making you nervous?" He seems so sincerely puzzled I can't help but laugh.

I wave an arm his way. "Are you kidding me? You're staring at me like Heidi Klum about to tell me whether

I'm in or I'm out. I'm not a supermodel, Jack. I'm not used to people watching me strut up and down the catwalk."

He frowns harder. "Isn't that show about fashion design? Not modeling?"

I cross my arms with a sigh.

"Okay, I hear you," he says, rising from his judgment chair. "Would it help if I walked with you? Maybe in front and you can shadow me until you feel more relaxed?"

"Maybe," I mumble, though I doubt I'm going to nail the signature Jack glide-prowl any time this century. But at least it will take his focus off of my body for a few minutes, hopefully giving me the chance to pull myself together.

"All right. Let's give it a go."

I follow him back to the starting point, wishing I weren't so aware of the way his broad shoulders make my tiny apartment feel even smaller than usual.

"Chest relaxed, not thrust out or caved in." Jack turns and starts down our improvised catwalk with me close behind, trying to imitate his utter ease in his body. "Let each step roll out after the next. No bounce, no sway, barely any effort."

My growl of frustration turns to a laugh as he spins to face me. "Stop. Don't look." I flap my hands. "I'm not ready for you to look."

"Is this helping?"

"Too soon to tell," I say. "But honestly, I'm not comfortable in my *own* body. Let alone Eric's. So, if you're looking for Vin Diesel-level of masculine perfection—"

"Wait." Jack frowns. "Vin Diesel is your idea of masculine perfection? Seriously?"

"Well, he's..." Actually, I've never given it much thought. But now that Jack's brought it up, I'm pretty sure my idea of masculine perfection is standing right here, towering over me with fiery green eyes and perfectly tousled hair and all the confidence one would expect from a guy who understands he's God's gift to womankind.

I clear my throat and avert my eyes, hoping my thoughts aren't showing on my face. "Just throwing out an example. My point is, you may need to adjust your expectations."

"Why?" His gaze sharpens, making me feel like he's looking right through me, seeing all my silly, embarrassing secrets. "Why aren't you comfortable in your own body?"

My shoulders bounce up and down beneath my suit coat as a wave of shyness prickles beneath my skin. "I don't know. I'm just..."

"Just what?" Jack eases closer, making my already elevated pulse gallop faster.

"I was never great at sports, I haven't been out dancing since college, and I spend most of my time alone in my apartment not touching other people," I say, my cheeks heating as I make my pathetic confession. "I'm not exactly leading a carnal existence. Unless you count my intimate time with a block of sharp cheddar before bed."

Jack doesn't say anything for so long that my flush becomes a full-fledged cheek-meltdown.

"Pretend I never said that," I finally say in a rush. "Keep walking. I'll keep following. I'll get it eventually."

"No more walking." Jack scrubs a hand across his jaw. "You still have your dad's old record player?"

I force my gaze to his, relieved to see he isn't looking at me like I'm the saddest cheese-binging loner in Loner Town. "On the bottom shelf, under the TV. Why?"

Jack doesn't answer. He circles my couch, crouches in front of the entertainment center, and makes a selection from my collection of vintage vinyl. A moment later, *Bring It On Home to Me* by Sam Cooke fills the room.

"May I have this dance, Miss Seyfried?" Jack stands, holding a hand out my way.

I shake my head with a flustered laugh. "You don't have to do that. Seriously, Jack, I—"

"Get over here, Eleanor." He crooks a finger. "We're going to get you comfortable in your own skin."

*Right. Because slow-dancing with a man who makes my heart beat out of my chest is such a* comfortable *experience.*

But I've made enough embarrassing confessions for one day. So I grit my teeth and cross the room, moving stiffly into position in front of Jack.

"Let's get rid of this." He reaches for my lapels, guiding my blazer off my shoulders, making the heart-pounding even worse as he tosses the coat onto the couch and wraps an arm around my waist. "I've never danced with someone in a suit."

"Which is why this is silly. I need to learn to walk like a man, not dance like a woman."

"You already know how to dance like a woman." Jack's arm tightens around me, making my breath catch as he takes control of the dance. "So dance with me. Focus on getting into your body and quit giving me lip."

"You're very bossy," I murmur as I glide one palm up to his shoulder.

"And you're very beautiful," he says, making my mouth go dry. "Which is part of the problem, Ellie. Even with the mustache and man-makeup, I can't believe other people don't see it."

"They don't," I say as Sam Cooke croons on. "Trust me, Jack. No one suspects a thing. I can do this."

"You can do anything you set your mind to." He draws me even closer, until my bound chest is inches from his and my fluttering stomach brushes against his belt buckle. I don't think I've ever been this close to Jack, and damn if I don't want to get even closer. "You're one of the most self-disciplined people I know."

"Thank you." I tilt my head back, holding his gaze, even though I shouldn't. If my eyes aren't giving me away already, they will sooner or later.

I've never been good at hiding the way I feel, and right now I'm feeling so many risky things. Attraction and longing and even more dangerous things like...gratitude. It's been so long since someone told me I was beautiful, and even longer since I knew they weren't just talking about the way I look.

"You're welcome." Jack's voice is low as he spins us both in a slow circle, his hips swaying so close to mine that for a moment I forget how to breathe. "But I'm not sure..."

"Not sure about what?" My head is spinning now, too. If I don't exhale soon, I'm going to pass out, but then Jack will probably catch me, and I can think of worse things than being scooped up in his arms.

Lots of worse things.

"I'm not sure I deserve your thanks." He stops swaying, but I barely notice. The flash of his sparkly green eyes has me totally off kilter.

And then he leans down, his lips moving closer to mine, and I realize several things all at once.

One: Jack is going to kiss me. This is not a drill. Repeat, this is *not* a drill.

Two: I didn't brush my teeth since I tossed back my morning espresso, and I probably have coffee bean breath.

Three: It's been six months since I've kissed anyone, and that was just Smith, my ex-boyfriend—who was only kissing me because our mutual friend Gregory was too busy to come drink with us and keep us from falling into stupid patterns that never work out because Smith is an overgrown child and I am done dating a man who plays Xbox twenty hours a week—and it is possible I've forgotten how kissing is done.

Four: I can't feel my arms. It's like the eighth-grade Christmas dance all over again. I'm under the mistletoe with Bradley Jones, and he's moving in, and I'm so overwhelmed that my nervous system is short-circuiting.

Except now I'm twenty-eight and there is no mistletoe, which means the gorgeous man about to press his lips to mine is doing so of his own free will. And, God, but he smells even *better* this close.

How on earth is that even possible?

My lips are parting to say something—possibly to ask about his delicious man scent or to blurt out an embarrassing confession about how long it's been since my last make-out session—when a hard knock on the door fills the silence.

Jack and I jump apart, and my breath rushes out with a shaky laugh.

"Door," I say, brilliant as ever. "I should get it."

"Yeah." He jabs a thumb over his shoulder. "I'll check the music."

We scatter in different directions, and I do my best to talk my lungs into functioning. But I'm still dizzy when I open the door to reveal Sonia standing on my welcome mat with a tiny brown bottle in her hand.

"Hey," she says with a grin. "Dad wanted me to run this down. He gave you the wrong glue. Did I hear Sam Cooke?"

"Yes, thank you." I laugh as I take the glue. "Sorry."

She frowns. "Sorry for what? Dad's the one who gave you the wrong bottle."

I shake my head, laughing some more because—anxiety. "Right. Sorry." I wince. "Sorry about the sorry."

"Oh-kay." Sonia arches a skeptical brow. "No big deal. Can I come in? Why don't you have your suit coat on? Do you need help?"

"So many questions you have," I mutter through clenched teeth.

"Now you're talking like Yoda." Sonia puts a hand on my forehead. "Are you sure you're feeling all right?"

"I'm fine," I say, praying Jack isn't overhearing all this. "But I—"

"I just remembered," Jack says, slipping past me on my left. "I have an appointment in SoHo at noon. Going to have to take a rain check on dude lessons." He stops beside Sonia, extending a hand. "Hi, I'm Jack. You must be Sonia. I've heard a lot about you. Love your work with Ellie's ringtone."

"Thank you." Sonia takes his hand and shakes it with a grin. "I do my best. I have a really embarrassing one queued up for next time."

"Excellent." Jack lifts a hand my way as he backs down the hall. "Sorry, Ellie. I'll text you, okay? See if we can hook up tomorrow? Maybe in the park? Somewhere with more space?"

"Oh. Okay," I stammer, forcing a stiff smile. "No problem. Just let me know."

"Will do." He punches the button by the elevator, relief illuminating his features as the doors slide open and he steps inside.

A second later he's gone. And I'm left standing in my doorway in semi-drag with a bottle of glue and a head full of unanswered questions.

"Did that really almost happen?" I ask, not realizing I've spoken aloud until Sonia says—

"Did he really leave? Yes. More important question, are you really okay? You felt warm, El."

*I bet I did*, I think, visions of that near kiss playing on endless repeat on my mental screen.

"I might need to lie down," I say. "Tell your dad thanks for the glue."

"Okay. Call us if you need something. Medicine or soup or whatever."

"Thanks, sweetie," I say as I close the door. I feel terrible for fibbing, but I can't very well tell a nine-year-old that I'm feverish with unrequited lust.

It *must* be unrequited, or Jack wouldn't have run out

of here like my couch was on fire. The near kiss was simply a moment of insanity brought on by exposure to sexy vintage Motown.

Or maybe I imagined it. Maybe it was all in my crazy head.

I absolutely *am* crazy because Jack is all kinds of off-limits. He always has been and always will be. He's my brother's best friend and business partner. Even if he were interested in me, getting my lips anywhere near his is a horrible idea that would end in disaster when we eventually parted ways. Company parties and family functions to which Jack has always been invited would be ruined forever, and I don't have enough friends or family members to alienate any of them.

I should assure him I can handle duding up solo, and make sure we're never alone together again.

Instead, when his text pops up a few hours later, I don't even try to resist.

*Meet me tomorrow in Central Park at noon? Southwest corner of the great lawn? No need to come in full Eric gear, but bring your improv sock. I'll bring lunch and we can practice manly eating after you master the walk.*

*See you then,* I respond. I force myself to leave it at that, grateful that they don't make an emoji for "I daydream about licking you an unseemly amount," and that I can go to sleep with my dignity intact.

For tonight, anyway.

# CHAPTER 7

## Jack

Day 5 Sunday 8/5

*I* love the Great Lawn.

Spanning fifty-five acres, this patch of pristine, sun-warmed grass has become my oasis, a breath of fresh air in an impossibly cramped metropolis.

Also, there's no bed.

More specifically, no chance of visualizing my best friend's sweet, sexy sister sprawled out on *her* bed, fists clutching her polka-dot comforter as I make her come in all the various ways I've been dreaming about lately.

Christ. I pulled a near all-nighter last night, finalizing an aggressive new portfolio package for one of our VIP NHL clients, but even that wasn't enough to distract me. By the time I dragged my ass out of bed for my morning run, I'd given up on evicting Ellie Seyfried from my mind.

Yesterday was a close call.

Too close.

The feel of her warm body melting against mine as we danced to Sam Cooke's soulful voice, her sharp intake of breath as my mouth lowered to hers, that damn bed mere inches away...

I close my eyes and tilt my face toward the sun, trying to burn that image from my retinas.

At least we'll be in public today, surrounded by the ultimate cock-block—tourists with selfie-sticks.

"You snooze, you lose, buddy." The voice is light and lovely, layered with a richness that can only belong to the woman who's taken up permanent residence in my head.

I open my lids and gaze into eyes the color of sapphires and a smile bright enough to compete with the sun. Ellie is already kneeling on my blanket, reaching for the goody bag I brought. Dressed in black jeans and a low-cut turquoise T-shirt, hair swept into a ponytail draped over her shoulder, she leans forward, granting me an unintentional peek at the curves beneath her shirt.

All traces of Eric Webb are gone.

My return smile is too eager, but it's too late to do anything about that now. "You made it."

"And *you* went overboard." She sits back on her heels, pulling out containers from the overstuffed bag: olives, cut fruit and veggies, three different hard cheeses, fig spread, four knishes, enough deli sandwiches to feed half the park, sparkling waters, and other snacks the owner at my favorite Jewish deli insisted I take when she heard I was meeting a woman for lunch.

*You have to spoil her, honey!* Ruth said. *Keep her coming back for more!*

"I wanted props for today's lesson," I tell Ellie now. "According to sociologists, eating can be an obvious gender marker."

Yeah, I'm *seriously* bullshitting my way through this one, but it's better than admitting the truth—that I love picnics in the park and wanted to do something fun with Ellie today so she wouldn't be so nervous about the dude stuff.

"But first," I press on, not giving her a moment to question my questionable science, "how's that walk coming along?"

She shimmies her shoulders, radiating newfound confidence. "According to Sonia, I nailed it."

"See! I told you it would get easier."

"She and Spence helped me out last night. I got dressed up again, and we did the catwalk thing in the hallway. It was very *Top Model*. Only—you know —manly."

"Pics or it didn't happen," I tease.

With a grin, she pulls out her phone, thumbs dancing across the screen. A few beats later, my phone buzzes with a text from a number I don't recognize.

"That'll be Spence with the evidence."

Grinning, I pull up the video her friend sent—Ellie strutting her stuff down the hallway in all her masculine glory.

"Nailed it," I say with a wink. "Want to do a few more laps around the park, just to be certain?"

"I hoofed it here from the Lexington stop." She drags the back of her hand across her forehead. "After hiking several long blocks with a balled-up tube sock chafing my thighs, I think I deserve some food."

"Here, here." This, from a random passerby, snickering as he continues across the lawn.

Ellie's ears turn red at the tips, but she giggles, a sound as contagious as her sunshine smile. I focus on that—the music of it, the way the skin around her eyes crinkles—anything to guide my thoughts away from the dangerous territory between her thighs.

"Now that I've announced my freak status to Central Park," she says, "are you going to teach me to eat like a man, or let me starve?"

Visions dance uninvited through my head—Ellie lying back against my chest, me feeding her olives, her tongue grazing my fingertips...

"God, yes," I say. Then clear my throat. "I mean, yeah. Let's dig in."

We get everything opened up and spread out on the blanket, and right away Ellie goes for the cheese, taking a dainty bite from a triangle of Manchego.

"Rule number one," I say, holding back a laugh. "No nibbling. You're a man-beast stockbroker ready to conquer the world, not a baby rabbit."

"Men don't chew their food before swallowing it?" She rolls her eyes. "So I should... what? Take the whole thing in my mouth? Swallow it down like a champ?"

*Oh Jesus, Ellie.*

I'm trying to be good. A stand-up gentleman who can spend an afternoon with a woman and not turn every comment into some kind of innuendo.

But I'm off my game, today and every day since Ellie Seyfried came back into my life with a nose for the story and an attitude that won't quit, no matter how many challenges she faces.

"Well?" she demands.

"Don't overthink it." I grab a piece of cheese and toss it back in a single gulp, doing everything in my rapidly waning power to stay on task.

Ellie gives me her judgy face again. "Did you even stop for a second to enjoy the complexity of the flavors? The salty tang, the creamy texture?"

"El. When you're shooting the shit with a bunch of filthy-rich jocks, it's hardly the time for cheese appreciation."

She dusts her hands together and shrugs. "Fine. The next time I find myself in a dick-measuring contest, I'll remember to skip the cheese. What else?"

We move on to the fruit and veggies, but no matter what I offer her, she insists on being mesmerizing, captivating, and so completely not-a-man that I'm ready to scrap the lessons, encourage her to eat her office meals locked in a bathroom stall where no one can see her, and ask her out on real date.

But then I remember the mission, and the stakes, and the fact that she's not out here today looking for a good time. She's out here because she's determined to finish her story, and she's counting on me to help her.

The sooner I get that through my thick head—*both* of them—the better.

"I didn't know what sandwiches you liked, so I got a bunch," I say. "Whitefish, smoked turkey with cranberry relish, roast tomato with pesto..."

"I'd love to try the smoked turkey, if that's okay?"

"No. It's not okay." I unwrap the sandwich and set it on her plate. "What you mean to say is, 'Let me get that smoked turkey,' or, 'Dibs on the turkey,' or 'The bird is mine, asshole.' Got it? Be assertive."

She scoffs. "That's not assertive. That's devolved."

"There's a fine line."

"More like a gulf." She lifts the sandwich with two hands and takes a small bite, chewing slowly before swallowing it down. "Anyone who thinks he needs to be a bully to get ahead in life is—"

"Realistic. I'm sorry, Ellie, but it's the way things are. If you don't want to be that guy? Fine. But you don't get ahead in this industry by being a decent human being."

"You and Ryan are decent. My father, for all his faults, is still a good man."

"I'm not saying everyone in finance is an asshole. But any time you're dealing with that much money and power, you get bullies and corruption and enough back-handed bullshit you wonder how you can drag your ass out of bed to face it another day. If you're going to jump into those waters, you need to be prepared."

"I don't buy that. It doesn't have to be that way."

"No, it doesn't," I agree. "But it *is* that way."

"Doesn't mean it can't change," she insists.

I shake my head, but she's already got me grinning again. There was a time I would've called Ellie's unwavering beliefs nothing more than blind hope or sweet naiveté. But now? No way. Ellie's not going into this with her eyes closed. She's simply determined to make the world a better place.

How could I not be on board?

"Well...that's why you're doing the story, right?" I ask. "To change something?"

She nods, taking another ladylike bite of her sandwich. "First I need to make people aware that something still *needs* changing. That we need to work harder and give this issue more than lip service."

"Exactly. And in order to do that, you need to play this part. Keep that in mind and don't shoot the messenger when I give you this next bit of advice." I reach for her hands and fold down her delicate pinkies. "You're not brunching with the queen. And you don't need two hands for a sandwich anyway. Just one-fist that bad boy. Take your filthy man-mitt and show that deli meat who's boss."

She rolls her pretty eyes but shifts the sandwich into one hand and mimics my moves.

"Better," I say with a nod. "You may think this is silly, but Rictor and his pals aren't dumb. If you don't walk the walk and eat the eat, you're gonna get made."

She hums as she looks out across the park, brow furrowed, the wheels in her head spinning so fast I can practically smell the smoke.

"I can see this is making you uncomfortable," I say. "If you'd rather come back to the office as yourself, as Ellie, we can find another position—real or fake. There has to be another way for you to get the scoop."

"Quitting is *not* an option. I just... Don't you see the irony?" She drops the sandwich onto her plate. "I'm taking pointers on how to be a guy for the sole purpose of infiltrating your company to research sexism and misogyny. And you're saying everything I do is too *feminine* for me to be taken seriously—from the way I walk to the words I use to how I chew. This kind of thing hurts *everyone*. Women should have equal opportunities in the workplace, and men should be able to eat cheese any way they want without other men threatening to tear up their man cards."

She rises onto her knees and reaches for the half-spent containers, ducking my gaze as she packs up the leftovers.

"Ellie. Please look at me." I reach for her wrist, my fingers circling it as I stroke her soft skin. When she finally sighs and meets my gaze again, I offer a tentative smile. "You're right. Everything you're doing at S and H... I feel like I've been asleep for years, then you show up and I haven't been able to catch a wink since. Just knowing that I've contributed to this, that I might have been unfair to the women in my life, even unintentionally..."

I shove a hand through my hair. Why can't I find the words? Why can't I tell her that I want to be better—that she's *making* me want to be a better man? And it's not just for the sake of her story, or because it's the right thing to do, or even because I'm into her and want her to trust me.

It's because she fucking inspires me.

I lost my parents when I was a junior in high school. In a single heartbeat—enough time for the guy in the car beside us to glance at his texts and swerve into our lane —my happy, carefree childhood was over.

Since then, life has done its damnedest to turn me into a jaded prick—hell, work in this soul-sucking industry long enough, and your heart will shrivel up even *without* the tragic backstory.

Yet Ellie makes me believe that things actually *can* change for the better.

But I guess my troglodyte DNA is the dominant

gene today, because all I manage to say now is, "You don't need my help. You're going to do a kickass job."

Ellie blows out a frustrated breath, but she relaxes. "What happened to, 'Welcome to Dude 101, insubordination will not be tolerated?'"

I lean back on the blanket and look up at the drifting clouds because if I keep looking at her I'm going to kiss her. And this time, I won't be able to stop, no matter who interrupts us. "I'm not exactly an objective source on this anymore, El. But for what it's worth? I think you're in good shape. Attitude goes a long way, and you're definitely—to quote our friend Rictor—in it to win it."

She laughs again, and I find myself ready to offer up my firstborn if it means I can keep hearing that sound.

Leaning back beside me, Ellie nudges my elbow with hers. "You really think so?"

"You're walking around Manhattan with a sock between your legs—that's dedication. And I don't know many people who could pull off a gender bend in the finance industry, *and* make friends doing it, yet you seem to have half the office eating out of your hand."

"My filthy man-mitt, you mean." Ellie turns on her side to face me, her head propped on her hand as she smiles. "I can't believe I'm sitting here feeling proud about how manly I am."

My gaze sweeps her face, taking in the delicate arch of her brows, the perfect slope of her nose, the curve of her lush, full lips.

Manly? Two days into our dude lessons, and she gets more beautiful every time I look at her. How on earth am I supposed to keep pretending she's not getting under my skin, drowning my senses, invading my every thought?

Fuck it. No more pretending. I want to kiss her. I *need* to kiss her, no matter how many people surround us, no matter how many warning bells clang in my head.

"Can I kiss you, Ellie?" I ask, voice husky.

Her blue eyes wide, and alive with a spark that melts my hardened financial sector heart, Ellie nods. But before I can make a move, she leans close, eradicating the distance between us.

Instantly, I'm lost in the taste of her kiss. There's no hesitation, only the intensity I've come to expect from her, mixed with a hunger that ignites things low in my body.

My hands slide into her hair, pulling her ponytail loose as she gasps into my mouth. I trace the outline of her lips with my tongue, teasing and tasting, breathing her in, committing every delicious second to memory.

The sounds of the city fade away—car horns and sirens and endless chatter—all of it muted until there's nothing left but the rush of my blood and a single word flickering through my mind.

*Perfect.*

She's perfect, exactly the way she is, no lessons required.

By the time we break for air, the sun has shifted to the other side of the park, and a cool breeze has chased off the less intrepid tourists.

Ellie holds my gaze, her lips red and swollen.

Neither of us says a word, and it truly is fucking *perfect*.

Until the spell breaks.

I see it the moment it happens, the sudden shift in her eyes from content to concerned.

Ellie sits up on the blanket, and I follow, trying to gauge a situation that has me unmoored. I'm out of my element, not sure what the right call is, only knowing that I want her to be okay.

"I... I'm sorry, Jack," she says, suddenly even more anxious than she was at her apartment yesterday. "This isn't... We can't..." She motions between us, nearly knocking over an open bottle of sparkling water, which I save before it topples into my lap. "This can't happen."

"It can't," I say, not sure if I'm agreeing or asking a question.

"Right. I mean...right?"

"Right." I wave a hand, as if to erase the last fifteen minutes. As if I could.

"Ryan texted to see what I was up to today," she says, "and I didn't tell him we had plans. That's weird, right? We're friends."

"We are," I say carefully.

"And adults."

"That, too."

"So why am I so nervous to tell Ryan about this? Well, not this..." She blows out a breath through pursed lips. "I don't mean *this*, like we're a thing. Which obviously we're not. I just meant—"

"Your brother thinks you have a crush on me."

"Wait. What? He told you that?" She glances my way for a split second, then dodges again, picking at a thread in the blanket. "Ugh! I'm going to murder him!"

"So, you don't?" I try not to sound deflated, but I'm not sure I'm successful. "Never?"

Ellie groans. "Fine, maybe I had the tiniest crush on you when you and Ryan were in grad school. But that doesn't count. You were my older brother's hot friend. That's textbook crush bait."

I fight the urge to grin, and lose. "So, you thought I was hot?"

"Must've been the drugs," she mumbles.

"That *one* time you smoked pot in your entire life."

"Pot has lasting effects, Jack."

I drag my thumb across my lower lip, the sweet taste of her still lingering. "So, back to the part about you thinking I'm sexy..."

She still won't meet my eyes, but behind the shimmering curtain of her hair, a shy smile plays on her lips. "Yes, you're good-looking. It's not like that's a secret. Unlike the location where I'm going to hide Ryan's body after I murder him in his sleep."

"Slow down there, Dexter." I laugh, nudging her knee with mine. "You know he loves you."

"I know. I love him, too, even when he's annoying me." Ellie sighs, pulling her knees to her chest and wrapping her arms around them. "Which is why I don't want to do anything to jeopardize his reputation. The same goes for yours."

I choose to believe she's talking about her article, and not that explosive kiss we just shared.

"I know what I signed up for," I say. "And Ryan and I both trust you to handle this appropriately, and to help us figure out where we went wrong so we can make it right."

"That...means a lot." She turns to me, her eyes guarded, but that shy smile still tugging at her lips. "I should probably go. I have things to take care of at home."

"Me, too." I reluctantly pack up the rest of our picnic gear. "I guess this means Dude 101 is over."

She flashes me a grin as we head out of the park together. "So that's it? I passed the course?"

"With flying colors." I give her shoulder a quick, totally appropriate, just-friends squeeze. "Skip the cheese platter, keep your sock stuffed in tight, and you've got this, El."

*And you've got* me, *wrapped around your dainty, sticking-up-in-the-air-when-you-eat pinky finger.*

It's true. Crushing on Ellie back in the day was one thing—something we apparently shared. Lusting after her was another. But now, after that kiss? After the way she made my heart slam against my ribs as the world spun away?

*This can't happen...*

Her words echo in my memory, and somewhere in the recesses of my mind, a door slams shut and bolts itself twice.

I try not to flinch at the finality of it.

She's right.

It can't happen. It *won't* happen.

And by this time next month, this whole mission will be nothing but a distant memory, shoved into a box with the Cheetos incident and dancing in Ellie's apartment and kissing her on the Great Lawn and the time I almost —*almost*—let down my walls with a woman who felt oh-so-perfect in my arms.

# CHAPTER 8

## Ellie

Day 6 Mon 8/6

*W*ith my rock solid new dude walk, acceptably masculine dining skills, and budge-proof mustache, come Monday morning, I should be feeling ten feet tall and bulletproof. And if that kiss in Central Park were removed from the equation, maybe I would be.

But the kiss is an unavoidable fact. The kiss happened.

I kissed Jack Edward Holt.

And he kissed me back. And it was the best kiss of my entire life, but we both agreed never to do it ever again.

Now I have to pretend that's no big deal while also pretending to be Eric the friendly stockbroker you want to confess your deepest, darkest work frustrations to.

I'm beginning to think I should have majored in theater instead of journalism.

Mercifully, the first familiar face I encounter is a friendly one. Lulu, looking as rosy and upbeat as ever in a pink silk shirt and black ruffled skirt, waves to me across the lobby and hurries over with a big grin.

"Good morning," she says, beaming at me as we head for the elevators. "Karaoke was so much fun on Friday! I'm glad you came."

"Me, too. It was the highlight of my weekend. Thanks for the invite."

She waves a breezy hand. "Any time. And who knows, maybe next time we can convince you to sing."

I smile just the right amount, barely disturbing my mustache. "Maybe. Now that I know your crew is kind to the tone-deaf."

"Absolutely. Kindness first. Laughs second. That's what I always tell my kids."

I step into the elevator, moving to the back to make room for the people behind us. "How many kids do you have?"

"Three wild little boys." Her eyes go wide as she blows out a long breath that ends in a laugh. "They were at their dad's this weekend. I used to get sad on his weekends, missing them, but karaoke changed all that. I also joined a book club."

"I love to read. What's your latest book club pick?" I ask, barely having to remind myself not to sound *too* enthusiastic.

I really am getting the hang of restrained corporate manliness.

Now if I can manage not to blush or stammer like a teenager with a crush when I run into Jack, I'll call this day a win.

We chat books up to the fifty-eighth floor and part ways at reception, Lulu heading to her desk on the far side of the room while I settle into my assigned spot among the other junior brokers. I make a mental note to ask Lulu how long she's been at the company and if she's ever applied for a management position, before diving into the emails waiting in my company inbox.

I'm digging deep on the portfolio specs for a potential client—a little shocked that Jack is trusting me to put together a proposal for a major league baseball player, considering my experience with real life finance versus business school financial theory—when a slim hand lands on my shoulder, making me jump.

"Hey there. Eric, right? Didn't mean to scare you." A tinkle of laughter fills the air as I turn to see S&H's hiring manager. Blair is wearing a tight red suit-dress with matching red lipstick and a smile far friendlier than anything I saw from her during my time in the office as Ellie. "I'm Blair Keneally. Sorry I didn't get to welcome you last week. Or vet you before your interview."

"Nice to meet you, Blair." Ignoring her subtle dig about my rapid hire, I take the hand she extends and shake it quickly, but firmly, hoping she won't notice how feminine my hands are. That's the one thing I can't change with makeup or glued on hair.

But Blair is clearly focused on other things. As soon as I release her hand, she leans in close, perching on the edge of my desk as she playfully wrinkles her nose. "I have to confess I get a little frustrated when wild cards knock my picks out of the park. But I'm sure we'll get along great. I have a good feeling about you, Eric." She cocks her head to one side, sending her silky blond ponytail sliding over one shoulder.

"Oh, um, well, thank you." I shift uncomfortably in my chair. Lulu and the other women in the office have been friendly, but this is the first time I've been on the receiving end of obvious flirtation.

She *is* flirting with me...

Right?

Ugh. Why? I mean, I guess I'm not bad looking if you like a lanky dude with a mustache, but I haven't been sending out any signals, and Blair doesn't seem like the type who goes for a Tom Selleck circa 1970 lookalike.

"You're so welcome." She reaches out, plucking a piece of lint from my shoulder and smoothing her fingertips across the fabric while I fight the urge to cringe. "In fact, I was wondering if you might be able to do me an *itty*-bitty favor. With all the vetting for the Portland office transition team, I'm behind on reviewing applications for New York. If I get you the files, could you handle that for me today?"

I pause, waiting for her to say she's kidding, that this is her standard first-week-at- the-office prank on the new guys. But she just keeps batting her perfectly made-up baby blues.

My first inclination is to help, but just as I'm about to offer it up, a voice in my head chimes, *WWDD— What Would Dudes Do?* A dude at my level wouldn't be so quick to take on extra work, no matter how flirty Blair's being.

I clear my throat. "I wish I could, but hiring isn't my area of expertise."

"Of course not. I just thought you might be able to look over these resumes and see if any stand out. I'd really value your out-of-the-box opinion on this."

I pretend to consider her request—I'd kill to get a look at those files. But something about her approach is making my sixth sense tingle—and not in the good way.

I shake my head, doing my best to appear sympathetic. "I'm pretty slammed myself. Jack's sent me enough new client profiles to have me staying late every night this week."

Her smile brittles. "We're all team players here, Eric. I'm sure Jack doesn't expect you to get everything done this week. He understands that priorities are flexible in a dynamic work environment."

Wow. I can't believe she has the ovaries to try to con me into doing her work. I'm about to apologize and offer another excuse, but then I remember that unnecessary apologies are on the dude no-no list. So, with a firm shake of the head, I follow up with, "No can do, Blair. Being the new guy, I think it's best if I stay focused on the work I've been assigned. I'm sure you understand."

Blair's pretty features scrunch into the "swallowed sour milk" expression I'm familiar with from Ellie's original attempts to get information from her, when Rictor breezes by, snapping his fingers, "On your feet, Webb. All hands on deck in the conference room."

"What's going on?" I ask.

"Dude." Rictor arches a brow. "Falling asleep on the job already? DOJ put a kill order on the Sparks-GenCom merger last night, and the tech sector is taking it in the ass. Jack wants your input."

"Be right there." Tamping down the zing I feel that

Jack requested my input, I flash Blair a "duty calls" smile and slip around her, laptop tucked under my arm, hoping there might be time to ask Jack how serious he wants me to get with my client research after the emergency huddle.

Is this just for show?

Or is he actually expecting me to put my incomplete MBA to work?

Either way, it's flattering to have been trusted with important research for the company he and my brother value above almost everything else in their lives. For my brother, I like to think family comes first, and I know Jack, an orphan since his parents died, is devoted to his friends.

But aside from that, it's all business all the time for those two.

That's the only reason Jack spent half his weekend with me, after all—because he was afraid I would drop the ball and negatively impact his business. It's something I would be smart to remember when I'm tempted to replay that kiss over and over in my mind like my favorite song.

Attaching meaning to a workaholic's moment of weakness would be foolish indeed.

I hurry into the conference room in a manly way I know would make Jack proud if he were watching, but he isn't. He's focused on something one of the senior brokers is showing him on his phone, his handsome features arranged into his all-business face.

The look remains as he calls the meeting to order with a quick, "Good morning, people. Looks like Monday's in the mood to kick our asses. So let's get right into it. We need to get ahead of the tech sector panic before our clients realize there's a reason to be nervous."

His attention skims the room, hesitating ever so briefly on yours truly before moving on with a smile. "Hannah will start us off with a recap of what went down last night. Hannah?"

I don't know whether to be disappointed or relieved that Jack is so clearly unruffled by what happened between us yesterday in the park. But I'm glad he's making good on his promise to give Hannah more responsibility. Not only has she got the room set up with coffee and healthy breakfast snacks, but she has a great handle on the merger situation, too.

Soon we're so deep in the market analysis weeds I don't have time to think of anything except scrambling to contribute as best I can.

"How is biotech reacting?" I lean back in my chair and spread my legs like I've seen the other guys do during these meetings. "If they're holding steady, we might be able to balance out some of the tech losses in that sector. We can also look at the foreign markets."

Jack holds my gaze a moment, and I try not to squirm beneath his intense green eyes. "You think this merger news will sink tech for the next quarter?"

"Not at all," I say confidently, surprised at how easily all of this is coming back to me. Just like riding a bike. Or kissing. Or kissing Jack...

*Focus, Ellie. Focus!*

"But this was a major merger," I continue, "and before today we had no reason to think it wouldn't sail through the regulatory proceedings. The market needs time to stabilize, and not all of your—*our*—clients have the patience for that."

Jack nods, though I'm not telling him anything he doesn't already know. I suppose he just wants to show the rest of the team I've got the chops to be here. "What do you suggest?"

"I have a few ideas for emerging stocks we can pitch the nervous investors," I say, "and I'm sure our client relations team can finesse the language on an email to ease everyone's minds. I don't anticipate S and H taking a big hit over this."

"You seem pretty confident," Rictor says. "For a guy who's been here all of a week."

I shrug. "There's an old saying about the stock market, Rictor. And at the end of the day, every one of our clients embodies it." I let out a low chuckle, gently stroking my mustache. "If you can't take the heat, stay out of the Street."

Okay, I totally made that up, but most of my colleagues are laughing, including Jack. Even Rictor's got a grin on his otherwise smarmy face.

"Agreed, Mr. Webb. Thanks for your, ah, *poetic* insights." Jack's lips twitch with a smile so subtle I wonder if I'm imagining it, before he turns his attention back to the room at large. "All right, people. Here's what we're going to do."

Jack is so confident and commanding, steering this ship through the uncertain waters of triple-dip recessions and market instability, that I'm hanging on his every word. There's something about a man in a crisp button-down with the sleeves rolled up, his strong forearms flexing as he writes on the whiteboard, taking control in a crisis.

I'm so sucked in that I don't budge from my seat until we're dismissed with our assignments. The moment I rise from my chair, the effects of the coffee Hannah so graciously kept flowing hit me all at once.

*Note to self: don't underestimate the power of a bold French Roast on your microscopic bladder.*

I cruise into the men's room only to stop dead at the sign hanging on the one and only stall—Out of Order.

"Shoot," I hiss, eyeing the three urinals on the wall, trying to imagine any way I might be able to make that happen.

I'm considering locking the main door to the bathroom when Frame and Wallace, two other junior account execs, push through it, talking animatedly as they head for the urinals. I turn toward the sinks, washing my hands as if I've already finished my business.

But I haven't finished, and the warm water rushing over my hands only intensifies the urgency building to critical levels behind my zipper. Trusting my gut—which says contorting myself into some insane position to align female anatomy with a male toilet isn't the best call—I make a break for my brother's office.

Yes, it's risky, but Ryan has a private bathroom, and right now privacy is of the utmost importance.

But when I reach Ryan's office, I nearly crash into the person rushing out of it.

Blair.

Her mouth presses into a firm line of pseudo-authority, but not before I catch the flicker of surprise—and guilt—in her eyes.

"Something I can help you with, Mr. Webb?" She

quips, narrowing her eyes in suspicion as if *I'm* the one who just got caught sneaking out of my superior's office.

I'm dying to know what she's up to, but I don't have time for her power games. One more minute and I'm literally going to explode.

"Just doing a few laps around the office to keep the heart pumping," I say, breezing past her with a chipper smile. "Sitting is the new smoking, Blair."

Jaw clenched and sweat breaking out on my forehead, I wiggle around the corner toward the senior executive lounge. There's a bathroom in there, and Eric is new enough to pretend he has no idea he isn't supposed to be trespassing in SeniorExecVille, right? I near the door and am about to reach for the handle when an older gentleman I vaguely recognize emerges with a delectable-looking sandwich.

Feigning great interest in my watch, I lean against the wall near the lounge door, cursing beneath my breath as I hear Rictor holding court from within about his Au Jus and roast beef sandwich preferences. If it were anyone else but him, I might be able to sneak in undetected.

But Rictor won't let this go. Rictor will shame Eric on principle, to show him his place, and not give a damn if Eric has irritable bowel syndrome or something that necessitates the use of a stall over a urinal.

Seriously, what are the rest of the underling men in this joint going to do if nature rings bell number two instead of number one?

I'm concerned for them, I really am, but at the moment I'm more concerned about peeing my pants.

Biting the inside of my cheek, hoping the pain will

distract from my bladder's banshee howl long enough for me to get downstairs to the street, buy a coffee, and get a token for the lavatory from the militant, bathroom-defending woman who runs Cup of Joes, I walk-squirm down the hall. I'm nearly to the T-intersection that will lead to the exit, when Jack swings around the corner.

The moment he sees me, his brows snap together in disapproval. He glances over his shoulder before crossing quickly to where I'm hugging the wall. "What's wrong? What happened to the walk? You were doing so well."

"That was before the only stall in the men's bathroom was broken," I whisper, toes squirming inside my too-large men's dress shoes as I clench my thighs together, briefly wondering how absorbent my tube sock really is.

Jack's eyes widen in immediate understanding. With another quick glance over his shoulder, he takes me by the upper arm, half dragging me down the hall, unlocking his door, and guiding me into his private office.

And there, across the room, near the floor-to-ceiling windows overlooking lower Manhattan, is the door to Jack's private bathroom.

Thank.

God.

Without another thought, I rush for the door, slamming it behind me as I flip on the light.

Several minutes later, I emerge from the bathroom limp with relief to find Jack leaning against his desk with an amused smile on his face.

"Better?" he asks.

"So much better." I sigh, shoulders sagging as my eyes roll heavenward. "Thank you."

"No problem. I put a call into maintenance about fixing the stall ASAP. In the meantime, use the senior exec lounge. I'll make sure all the guys on the team know it's free for their use."

"Thanks again," I say, sufficiently recovered from my emergency to become aware of the fact that Jack and I are alone. Very aware. And also a little nervous. "So, um, good meeting this morning."

"Yeah," he says, lips curving on one side. "You're killing it, El. Are you sure you don't want to come work for us for real? Give up the glamorous life of a work-at-home journalist and help us make even more ridiculous amounts of money?"

"Ha! Um, no..." I smile too wide but figure it's acceptable to let my guard down now that we're alone. "But I'm flattered. And glad I haven't let you down."

"No, you haven't," he says, sobering. "But what about things on your end? How's the broker workload meshing with your article sleuthing?"

"Fine. Though I'd like access to Blair's records if possible. My sixth sense is tingling... She tried to pawn off her workload on me this morning." I give a small shake of my head. "She said she wants my outsider's perspective on potential candidates, but something about it felt like a set-up. Or at least a test."

"Yeah, she doesn't usually ask brokers for hiring input." Jack runs a hand through his wavy hair, and I can't help but flash back to the park yesterday. His lips on mine. My fingers sliding into those silky locks...

"Blair's a good manager, though," he insists, pulling me out of my reverie.

"If you think so." I swallow the urge to tell him about spotting Blair in Ryan's office. For all I know, she has every right to be in there, and I don't want to sound like a petty underling with a grudge.

"My guess is she's miffed about me fast-tracking your hire and is looking for a fight," Jack says.

"Let's hope she doesn't look too hard. My credentials are a joke, Jack."

"Not true." He gives me a conspiratorial wink. "I've made the necessary adjustments to your personnel file. On paper, you're legit."

"Still. I'd rather fly below the radar with Blair."

Jack offers a sympathetic smile. "Her focus on you will fade soon enough—she's got a lot of other priorities. But if you can gain her trust, she'd be a good resource."

"I have plenty of resources," I say.

"You may have made some friends, but no one knows the inner workings of S and H like Blair. It's why she has a corner office and six weeks' paid vacation. Woman knows her stuff."

I cock an eyebrow. "Does she know she's making less than her male counterpart on the west coast...who's dealing with a significantly smaller staff and has less experience and education?"

Jack leans back against his desk, folding his arms across his muscled chest. "Do I even want to know how you came by that information?"

"Probably not. But if I'm going to prove this is a widespread issue, I need more than hearsay. I really would like to peruse her files, to see who's applied for various positions and who's been granted interviews— not just management, but all levels."

"What are you hoping to find?"

"Just following up on a hunch, looking to connect a few dots. I'm not going to publish confidential information—nothing that links back to individual employees. You could even strip out names—I'm only interested in gender. And I don't need discipline records or worker's comp claims or anything like that. Do you think you could make those files available to me? I'd rather not have to suck up to Blair, if I don't absolutely have to."

He nods as he stands, moving away from his desk. "All right. I'll need to run a script to pull out personal identifiers, but I can get you what you need." He glances at his watch and lets out a sigh. "But I won't have time until after closing bell. Can you stay late?"

"Sure." I follow him to the door and head back to my desk, trying not to feel disappointed that things are so... normal between us.

*What were you expecting, El? A red-hot make-out session after the morning meeting?*

No. Normal is good. Now I don't have to worry about one silly kiss messing up our friendship or Jack's relationship with my brother.

Everything is great. I'm carrying my weight as Eric, getting good material as Ellie, clicking with most of my team, and I even manage to grab a sandwich from the break room before they're all gone. It's pimento cheese, however, so I opt for a crust-nibble and toss the rest in the trash.

Unless it comes in a bag and goes crunch, cheese was never meant to be *that* processed or pimento-ed.

I have strong opinions about treating cheese with the dignity it deserves, and therefore I am starving by the time five o'clock rolls around. By six, my stomach is pitching a fit, but Jack's office door is closed and there are serious hard-at-work murmurings from behind it, so I cruise back into the break room. But the organic snack machine does not care for my credit card—it probably heard I eat Cheetos and is being judgmental—and without my purse I have nowhere to scrounge for change.

"Oh, cruel world," I mutter, sagging back against the wall.

I'm being dramatic, of course, but by seven o'clock, the hunger pains aren't funny. Neither is the lightheadedness or the cramping in my hollow stomach. Finally, I'm forced to knock on Jack's door.

He answers with his phone to his ear and holds up one finger.

I shake my head and mouth, "Starving." My stomach echoes the sentiment with a long growl. Jack nods, holding up that single finger again before retreating to his desk.

What happens after that is a bit of a blur, but the next thing I know, I'm sitting on the floor outside his office and Jack is shaking me awake with a worried frown. "Ellie? Jesus, are you okay? You scared me."

"What happened?" I ask, head spinning as I focus on Jack's face.

"You slid down the wall." His fingers curl around the back of my neck in a way that makes me even more lightheaded. "I think you passed out. Did you eat anything at all today?"

I smack my lips a couple times, trying to remember. "Not since breakfast."

Jack scowls. "Why not? What were you thinking?"

"I was thinking that pimento cheese is vile, and the snack machine wouldn't take my card." I frown back at him. "I'm used to working right next to my fridge. It's a learning curve."

He shakes his head with a sigh. "And you're not used to working for a slave driver who keeps you at the office all night. This is my fault. Come on. We're getting you food. Stat."

"But what about—"

"I can access the company database from my place. We'll get Chinese to go, make sure you have enough fuel to keep from passing out, and I'll print the records for you before you head home." I start to protest, but Jack cuts me off with a hand held in the air. "I insist. I'm not sending you out into the streets like this. If you pass out on a subway platform and something happens to you, I'll never forgive myself."

I shudder. "I have nightmares about passing out on the subway platform and smelling like pee for the rest of my life."

Jack cracks up, the sound of it filling me with longing. "All the more reason you're coming home with me. My apartment is a pee-free zone. At least the, uh... Okay, not sure where I was going with that." He offers his hand to help me up, his smile tentative. "So. You, me, Chinese, files?"

"Okay." I try to ignore the warmth filling my chest. But by the time Jack helps me to my feet, keeping his arm around me as he leads the way to my desk to fetch my briefcase, the warmth has spread.

And the reason for the warmth is Jack's touch and his concern and the way he stays close as we hit the street, clearly not caring what any passersby might think of him having his hand on another man's back. The reason is the supersize crush I'm developing, which only gets worse when Jack proceeds to order an obscene amount of Chinese food in the name of "giving me leftovers to take to work tomorrow."

A man who kisses like the world's about to end, is amazing in a crisis, *and* is serious about making sure I'm fed?

Be still my beating heart...

But it won't be still. That's my problem, and the reason I should take my food and go home—do not go up to his place, do not risk being alone with Jack again.

Instead, I let him hold the door open for me and follow him to his elevator because some things—like men as smart, thoughtful, and drop-dead sexy as Jack Holt—are impossible to resist.

# CHAPTER 9
## Jack

Day 6 Monday 8/6

"*T*his view is incredible!" Ellie leans close to the floor-to-ceiling window in my living room, peering out across the city. De-mustached and makeup free, she's dressed in one of my well-worn Harvard sweatshirts and a pair of basketball shorts about five sizes too big on her, but it's the best I could offer, considering she was dying to get out of her man-suit and I don't keep a stash of ladies' clothes on hand.

I'm not gonna lie. Seeing Ellie in my clothes, knowing there's nothing between the fabric and her skin? That image will get me through more than a few lonely nights.

"If I lived here," she says, still gazing out the window, "I'd never leave this spot. You'd have to hire a maid to dust and water me once in a while. It's that beautiful. Don't you think?"

The sun went down an hour ago, leaving the glass

and steel of Manhattan bathed in a muted glow. But I'm not looking at the buildings or the pink sky or the latticework of roadways below. Not anymore.

Yes, I appreciate the view my open-plan penthouse apartment affords. It's glorious day or night, summer or winter, rain or shine.

But it doesn't compare to the view tonight, the warm light shimmering in Ellie's dark-chocolate hair, the endless sounds of the city muffled by the glass and the funky jazz playlist drifting from my speakers.

"Beautiful," I say softly. I hold up her coffee mug, steam curling from the surface. "Dash of cream, teaspoon of sugar, yes?"

Ellie smiles, my reward for getting her coffee order right, and I hand over the mug.

Dinner was easier. We were both starving, she was still mustached and manly, and we dogged the Chinese takeout straight from the containers, barely stopping for air.

But now she's fresh-faced and glowing, my clothes draped over her curves, her dark hair spilling across her shoulders, begging to be touched. And coffee? That's one step closer to dessert, which, as far as I'm concerned, is one step closer to sex, which is almost certainly a terrible idea.

Almost...

Certainly...

Ellie closes her eyes and takes the first sip, letting out a moan that goes straight to my dick.

*Fuck me.*

"Oh, Jack. Where have you *been* all my life?" She moans again, showing absolutely no consideration for what she's doing to me. "I had no idea you could make coffee like this."

"One of my two talents," I say.

Ellie raises a brow. "What's the other one?"

*Tearing off those shorts and burying my face between your thighs until you forget what fucking planet you're on...*

I hold her gaze a moment longer, lost in the dangerous dream of what it might feel like to go down on her, to hear her scream my name, to feel her hands rake through my hair as she pulls me closer...

"Fine, don't tell me." Her playful laughter drags me back to the moment.

"Actually, there isn't another one." I step to the side, putting some much-needed distance between us, hoping she doesn't notice the bulge in my pants. Unlike Ellie, I'm still wearing my all-too-confining work clothes, and my cock is hating me for it. "I'm really only good at the coffee. Probably why I'm still single."

"Somehow I doubt that." She smiles again.

Forget that million-dollar view. I could stand here and watch this woman wear my clothes and drink my coffee and laugh at my dumb jokes forever.

And if it weren't for her brother, and the necessary boundaries of professionalism, and the fact that I have to interact with her daily without dragging her into the closest break room and devouring her lush mouth, I'd probably tell her as much.

Alas...

"That script should be done parsing the personnel data in about half an hour," I say instead, smooth talker that I am. "Then we can print the files, go through everything with a fine-toothed comb, and see where we're at."

"Really?" Ellie lights up, but then shakes her head, a frown pulling at her perfect, pink lips. "You don't have to do that, Jack. I can take the files home. There's a reason they call it investigative journalism. We investigate. All part of the gig."

"I have a stake in this, too, remember? Besides—I know my employees. This will go a lot faster if you ask me questions as they arise."

"Well, thank you. I appreciate the help. And access to the files. And the dinner and coffee." She downs the last of it then heads into the kitchen with her mug. "And basically everything you're doing for me, when all *I'm* doing is making your job harder."

*You're making something harder, all right...*

"Every business has growing pains." I follow her into the kitchen and drop our mugs into the dishwasher. "I'm grateful you're here to help us through ours. You were right during your fake interview—S and H needs you."

This gets another smile. "You sure I'm not bringing down the property value around there? I know I talk a good game, but I'm not exactly the Wolf of Wall Street."

"Come on. A little more training, some on-the-job experience, your real identity... You'd be unstoppable. I meant what I said—there's a place for you at Seyfried and Holt if you ever want to change tracks."

She lifts a wry brow. "Something tells me that partner of yours would disagree."

"Not if he saw you in action."

"He can't, though. That's the thing." She blows out a breath and leans back against the kitchen counter, glancing toward the big windows in the living room. The jazz playlist that entertained us through dinner finally wraps up, and in the silence that follows, the mood feels suddenly heavy.

"I talked to Ryan last night," she continues. "I gave him an update on my story, but I left out so many details. Major ones." Her eyes flick to mine for a second, heat gathering between us. "I hate lying to him."

Guilt simmers in my gut, and I fight the urge to take her face into my hands. To kiss her. To give her an entire red-hot night of details we'll never be able to tell her brother about.

On the verge of making a move I can't take back, I busy myself with the dishwasher. "It won't be much longer. Soon you'll be able to show him your findings and tell him the whole sordid, fake-mustached tale. He'll have no choice but to bow down to your superior sleuthing skills."

*After he kicks my ass for letting this happen.*

"You're probably right," she says, but from the corner of my eye I catch her shaking her head, absently playing with the ties on her borrowed basketball shorts. "But sometimes I feel like I'm living someone else's life. I know I made the choice to switch gears in grad school, but even with all the catching up I had to do in the journalism program, I still thought it might work out."

"Hasn't it?"

"Not exactly." Ellie shrugs. "I had this whole life plan —go to school, get a great job in business, make a ton of money, make my dad proud." Her voice is so quiet, it feels like she's making a confession.

"Instead, I'm in a studio apartment in Astoria," she

continues. "My dishes rattle every time the train goes by. I have a master's degree from a prestigious university, but most days I'm writing puff pieces like 'Ten Signs He's Just Not Into You' and 'Is Your Smoky Eye Setting Off the Right Alarms?'"

Dishwasher forgotten, I step in front of her and put my hands on her shoulders, offering an encouraging smile. "I have no idea what a smoky eye is, but I *do* know that whatever you're working on, you put your all into it. That's what counts."

"It's not serious work, though. The S and H story is the first time in my professional life I'm working on something that matters. Something that can help people."

"It *will* help people. It's already helping."

"That's what I thought, too," she says. "The story, the work... I'm not even close to finished, and I already believe it's the most important thing I've ever done."

"That's a good thing, no?"

"Maybe it would be, if I were doing it as myself." She blinks and turns away, but not before I catch the tears glistening on her cheeks. "All those smart, fearless things you think I can do? I can't seem to do them without a costume and a mask. Without pretending I'm someone else. You think I'm this badass writer who goes after what she wants, but most of the time...I'm just scared."

My heart cracks right in half. "What are you afraid of?"

"Not mattering. Wasting the time I've been given. Looking back in twenty years and wishing I'd done everything differently."

She looks so vulnerable—the fear etched in her eyes,

the downward turn of her mouth, the furrow between her brows—some primal instinct claws its way out of my chest, and all I can think about now is how badly I want to protect her. How much I want to take away her pain.

How desperately I need her to see herself the way I see her.

I cup her face in my hands, brushing away her tears with my thumbs. "This is only the beginning for you. You're fierce and talented and smart as hell—with or without the costume. Personally, I haven't been able to get you out of my mind for a second in weeks."

"That's only because I've infiltrated your workplace, passed out in front of your office, and—"

"No. It's because you inspire me. Because you're an amazing human being." I hesitate a beat, but I can't hold back the rest of the words desperate to make their way out. "And because, ever since we kissed, all I can think about is how badly I want to kiss you again."

Her breath hitches. "You do?"

"I was so zoned out today, Rictor told me go home and sleep it off." I slide my thumb across her lower lip. "I'm still thinking about it, El. Right now."

"Me, too," she whispers, breath as soft as powder.

"Good to know." I lean down, bringing my lips to hers, but it's nothing like our first kiss.

This kiss is hungry, starving, almost *savage*.

Her hands twist into the front of my shirt, and I grab her around the waist and lift her onto the countertop, shifting between her thighs. She tastes like creamy coffee and cinnamon and raw, unfiltered Ellie, and if I drop dead right here, her legs wrapped around me, her hands on my chest, I'll say it was a life well lived.

She moans against my lips, driving me wild.

I need to touch her, to feel her against my skin. All of her.

I slide my hands up her outer thighs, warm and silky-smooth inside the borrowed shorts, and she inches forward on the countertop until I've got a handful of her firm, perfect ass.

But it's not enough. Not for either of us.

"More kissing, less clothes?" I ask, voice rough with need.

"Fewer," she pants.

"What?"

"It's *fewer* clothes, not less. Although you could say 'less clothing.'"

"I have an idea. Fewer clothes, fewer interruptions from the grammar police, and more time for coming our brains out."

"Brilliant." Ellie laughs, kissing me again. She slides off the counter, and we stumble into the bedroom together, stripping as we go, crashing onto the bed in a tangle of bare arms and legs, Ellie's dark brown hair a stark contrast against my white duvet.

Finally freed from the confines of my dress pants, my rock-hard cock throbs against her damp thighs, but I'm not about to rush things with Ellie. I want to take her in, kiss by kiss, one sexy moment at a time.

I start with her collarbone, blazing a trail of kisses from one shoulder to the other, then down to her breasts. She gasps my name, her back arching as I suck one of her tight peaks into my mouth, but I don't stop, sucking her harder, grazing her with my teeth, pushing her to the edge before turning my attention to the other breast, every movement driving her wild. I can't get enough of her, my senses overloaded by the silk of her skin, her taste, the way she writhes beneath me.

I can't wait another minute. I need to make her come.

I drag my mouth down her stomach, tracing a path between her thighs, slowly guiding her legs apart. My tongue swirls over her clit, and Ellie threads her hands into my hair.

"Oh, God," she moans, nails digging into my scalp.

It's all the invitation I need.

I grab her thighs and slide my tongue inside her. Her taste is intoxicating, flooding my mouth as she arches her back and rocks her hips against my kiss. I'm drunk on her—her scent, her toned thighs, the moans she makes as I fuck her with my mouth.

"Jack," she breathes, fisting my hair, and I know she's right on the edge.

That she trusts me to take her there.

It's a gift, and I still can't believe she's offering it to me. Here. Now. In my bed.

I suck her clit between my lips, licking and teasing, stroking her until she shatters, screaming my name.

Slowly, reverently, I kiss her thighs, her belly, those beautiful breasts, working my way back to her mouth. Her cheeks are flushed and her eyes dark with desire.

"More," she whispers, arching against my cock. Her heat is a siren call I'm powerless to resist. I grab a condom from the nightstand drawer, rolling it on as I tease her entrance.

"Please," she says. "I need you inside me."

*God, Ellie.*

We've crossed so many lines tonight, but not this one. Not yet. Five more seconds, and there's no going back.

"Are you sure?" I ask, every inch of me pulsing with need for this woman. "Absolutely sure?"

"I'm *so* sure." Ellie curls her fingers around my shoulders, pulling me down for another kiss as I slide blissfully inside her, one inch at a time. And *God* maybe I really did die back there in my kitchen. That has to be it. Because right now my body is on fire, my brain has liquefied, and the last thing I know for sure is that nothing in this world has ever felt as much like home as this woman.

I try to make it last, to draw out every moment of bliss, but the second Ellie goes again, arching into my cock as her body locks tight around me, I'm gone.

I explode, my body humming with electricity, pleasure, and something deeper.

Something I'm not sure I have a name for, but it makes the moments we spend curled up in each other's arms some of the sweetest in memory.

"You sure you don't want to stay?" I ask, walking her out as the car service rolls up in front of my building a few hours later. "We could grab some breakfast on the way to the office tomorrow, chat about those files. Sal's diner makes a mean veggie omelet."

"I'd love to, but all my Eric stuff is at home," Ellie says. "I can't get ready without it."

"You can borrow one of my suits. We'll roll up the cuffs, eighties style."

Ellie laughs, but I can tell my powers of persuasion are failing. "If I stay, you'll keep me up all night, and then I'll fall asleep during the morning meeting and get in big trouble with my boss."

"You've got me there," I say. "Your boss *is* kind of a dick."

She smiles. "Honestly, I'm more worried about Blair. That woman has a lady boner for policies and procedures, and as far as she's concerned, Eric Webb is breaking every one of them."

"Not *every* one. I happen to know for a fact S and H has a very liberal policy on consensual interoffice relationships."

"Hmm. I'll keep that in mind." Ellie turns toward the waiting car, but I stop her, pulling her back into my arms. I lean close, breathing her in once more.

*I could get used to this...*

"Tomorrow's gonna be brutal," I confess.

"Only until everyone else leaves for the night."

"Oh, really?" I nudge her nose with mine, loving this flirty, playful side of her. "What happens then?"

The look in her eyes sends a fresh bolt of desire straight to my dick.

"Why, then, Mr. Holt..." She nips my earlobe then whispers against my neck, giving me another instant hard-on. "We meet up in your office, lock the door, and take full advantage of my employer's liberal interoffice relationship policy."

# CHAPTER 10

## Ellie

Day 7 Tues 8/7

*T*he world is no longer what it was.

The universe has shifted on its axis, and neither I, nor it, will ever be the same.

I float to the train on the wings of last night's multiple orgasms and sit staring out the window with a goofy smile that not even the guy next to me—the one whose aggressive hacking portends contagious doom to all in his vicinity—can wipe away.

Before the Evening of Life-Altering Sexy Times, I was aware that my sex life had been average at best, a real snooze-fest at worst, but I had no idea just how behind the curve I'd been. I hadn't realized my body was capable of the magical things Jack coaxed from it with his kiss, his touch, his gloriousness moving inside me until my every cell screamed *Hallelujah*.

I have been ruined for other men.

Absolutely *ruined.*

And yet, I still can't.

Stop.

Smiling.

I may be ruined, but I'm going to enjoy my continued ruination for as long as it lasts.

Because it's going to happen again. I may not have rearranged Jack's reality the way he reordered mine, but I could tell he felt the combustible connection, too. It was mutual, and there's no way either of us can walk away from that after a single taste, no matter how much we have to lose. An office romance is risky enough when one party isn't the other party's best friend's little sister and an undercover reporter dressed in drag.

Jack and I are going to have to be careful. Very, very careful.

That in mind, I pause near the decorative pillars outside the S & H building, drawing caution close and wrapping it around my head and shoulders like my favorite hoodie, doing my best to conceal my soaring, giddy inner joy. I lock away my just-got-laid-by-the-King-of-Orgasms grin in the nick of time.

I've just patted my mustache down over my newly calm lips when Lulu bursts from the lobby doors, hustling down the street in my direction.

I lift a hand to say hello, but the tears glittering in her eyes make it clear this isn't the time for morning pleasantries. "Lulu. Hey. Are you all right?"

She shakes her head, glancing over her shoulder before coming to join me where I'm tucked between two faux pillars carved into the edifice of the historic building. "Caleb's school called. He threw up his morning snack again, and I have to go pick him up."

"I'm sorry. I hope he feels better."

"Oh, I'm sure he feels fine." She lifts her eyes to the sky and swipes a finger beneath her lashes, catching a tear. "Caleb is a super picky eater. Anything new activates his gag reflex. I've tried to tell his teacher that, but she won't stop pushing him to try new foods, and the school has a zero-tolerance policy for kids getting sick. This is the third time this month I've had to leave to get him, and my supervisor is *not* happy. Will doesn't care that I get all my work done as soon as I get home. Every time it happens, he gets more frustrated. But my ex refuses to share pick-up duty on my days, and I don't have anyone else."

She pulls in a shaky breath, fresh tears rising in her eyes. "If I lose this job, I'll be underwater in less than a month. It's impossible to put anything into savings with three kids under the age of nine."

I put a gentle hand on her shoulder, willing strength into her petite frame. "I'm so sorry, Lulu. I know some of the old guard can be ridiculous about working from home. Maybe that's something the company should address from the top down? Is there a place where employees can anonymously suggest policy change?"

Lulu shakes her head. "The last woman who complained about the attitude toward mothers in the office was out in a month."

My lips part to tell her that's bullshit, and that I'm going to bring this up with Jack and Ryan personally, but of course I can't say that.

I'm *Eric*, not Ellie, and I need to stay undercover if I want to get the rest of my scoop.

And I need that scoop, not just to please my editor Denise, who is completely psyched about the new direction for my article, but to do right by the people working for my brother and Jack. And the best way to prove my good intentions is to keep my secret.

At least for now.

So I furrow my brow and nod sympathetically. "I get it. But if there's anything I can do, let me know."

Lulu pats my arm. "You're sweet. You're going to do great here, I know it. We've got a few rotten apples in the office, but the big bosses are great guys. Keep it up and you're going to impress the hell out of them."

It's good to hear. And it makes me feel awful at the same time.

I hate lying to Lulu—to anyone, really.

By the time I make it to my desk, my giddy has vanished, replaced by concern about what I'm going to do when it comes time to show my cards. Eventually, anyone who reads my article will know that Ellie and Eric are one and the same.

What will Lulu and the rest of the people in the office I'm coming to respect and care about think of me then? Will they understand why I lied? Will they realize how much I truly want to be a catalyst for positive change?

Or will they hate me for being a nosy journalist?

All of these worries are still swirling in my head when a floral-sugar-citrus scent envelopes me from behind, signaling the arrival of my very nice-smelling nemesis.

"Hey there, workaholic. What time did you get out of here last night?" Blair asks, tapping a shiny nail on my desk.

If I didn't know better, I'd swear there was a spark of challenge in her eyes, and my brain swirls with a new batch of panicked questions. Did she see me outside Jack's office last night, passed out like a helpless wimp? Did she hear him call me Ellie? Watch as he practically carried me out the door? Has she seen the "girlfriend got laid" glimmer in my eye and put two and two together to identify me as a reporter in drag who's banging her fake boss?

Is my cover completely blown?

Taking a deep breath and attempting to remain calm, I say, "Not too late. Maybe around seven. You?"

"Oh, I was here until midnight going through those personnel files. Speaking of which..." Her talon *tap tap taps* again, right next to my laptop. "I took a peek at yours, and I noticed a few, shall we say, discrepancies."

"Discrepancies?" My voice breaks, but I clear my throat and soldier on, ignoring the pounding of my heart. "Well, I'm happy to talk with Jack about that. I thought we had everything in order, but I'm sure I can help fill in any gaps."

She purses her lips, pondering my words. My *lies*.

Filthy, filthy lies. God, I'm so bad at this!

"It's nothing we need to bug Jack about." She pats the lapel of my suit coat, batting her eyelashes again. "I just noticed that you don't have your Series Seven and Sixty-three licenses yet. Is that correct?"

I consider lying but think better of it. "That's

correct. But I'm planning to take the exams. As soon as possible."

"I should hope so. You'll need to put that to bed before you start trading on behalf of clients."

I nod. "I think Jack's idea was for me to get the lay of the land and then transition into a more active role with clients."

"Of course." She flashes a smile, and I try not to sigh in relief. But then she scrunches up her passive-aggressive nose. "It's just that, given your level of experience with Hannaford Capital, I'm surprised you don't already have your licenses. Was your last firm aware of that?"

"I had more of an analyst role there." My gaze darts around the office in search of a savior, any savior. Barb from accounting? Hannah? Jack? Heck, I'd take Rictor riding my ass at this point, but he's nowhere to be seen.

"Listen, Eric. I need you to make this a top priority. If finances are an issue for you," she says, scanning my slightly off-kilter suit, "I'm sure Jack wouldn't mind authorizing S and H to cover the fees."

"Really? That's generous." Sensing my chance to turn the tables, I tap a fist on the desk. "And pertinent. I've been wondering how the selection process works for something like that."

Blair narrows her eyes, but if she suspects I'm up to something, she doesn't show it. "No process. Just a perk of the job."

"For anyone who wants to take the exams?"

"Well, not just anyone. But for those who show promise and ambition? You bet." She leans in close and lowers her voice, as if we're sharing a secret. "Something tells me you won't have any trouble getting it authorized."

"But who determines which employees show promise?" I press. "What if someone on the support team is interested in furthering her career, but doesn't have a chance to show her skills in action, and therefore can't be evaluated for these kinds of perks?"

Before Blair can reply, Hannah appears on my other side.

"Hey, Eric, Blair." Hannah nods at the other woman before her focus returns to me. "I hope I'm not interrupting, Eric, but we could use you in the executive lounge."

"We're done here. No worries," Blair says, backing away with a smile most people wouldn't consider menacing. But I'm getting to know Blair, and to know her is to be wary of everything about her.

Especially her smiles.

Hannah sighs in relief. "Oh, good. Jack is tied up with another client, and his nine a.m. is early. Walker Dunn plays pro hockey for the Buffalo Tempest. Jack said you know enough about the game to keep him entertained until he can take over?"

"Absolutely." I rise from my desk chair, fighting the urge to bound down the hall like a kid on the way to get her puck signed. "I'm a huge Tempest fan. Not to mention a Walker Dunn fan. His face-off stats are incredible."

Hannah smiles. "Perfect. Sounds like he'll be in great hands."

But will he, I wonder? I have no doubts about my ability to make small talk with a player I admire, but are my hands really great for this company? Jack and Ryan said they want to get to the bottom of any disparities in the way their employees are treated, but are they ready to deal with the wide variety of not-okay practices I'm uncovering?

And what about the consequences of what happened last night?

Of Jack's mouth on mine, and the reality-altering things he made me feel? Of the way he listened when I got sucked into the deep waters of quarter-life crisis, and how he made me feel not-at-all alone?

What about the thrill that shoots through my entire being simply because I'm passing by his office and catch the muted murmur of his sexy-as-sin voice through the closed door?

I have no idea.

But one thing I do know for sure—the chances of my emerging unscathed from this experience are getting smaller with every passing minute.

# CHAPTER 11

## Jack

Day 7 Tues 8/7

RYAN: How's your new broker working out. Webb, right?

JACK: Yeah. Webb's an asset for sure. Knows his stuff. Already adding value. And everyone likes the guy, to boot.

RYAN: Good. Looking forward to meeting him when I'm back. And our girl?

JACK: Our girl?

RYAN: My sister? The one you're supposed to be keeping an eye on? Sounds like things are getting intense with her research.

JACK: Define intense.

RYAN: She mentioned issues with our hiring and promotions, and some other staff discrepancies. Promised she'd give me the full play-by-play when I'm back in the office, but something tells me this story's getting bigger than she expected.

JACK: You think she can't handle it? Because let me be the first to disabuse you of that notion. She's on it, Ryan, like you wouldn't believe.

RYAN: Didn't say she couldn't handle it. Just wondering what kind of fallout I need to prepare for once that bomb drops.

JACK: Ellie's not going to drop any bombs. She's a pro. Yeah, we've got some issues, and she won't shy away from reporting on them. But she won't rake us over the coals.

RYAN: You seem to have her all figured out.

JACK: You're the one who told me to keep an eye on her. Give her what she needs.

RYAN: Is that what you're doing?

JACK: What do you mean by that?

RYAN: Exactly what I said. Dude, relax. Why are you so squirrelly today?

JACK: Sorry. Prepping for a big meeting with Walker Dunn. Actually, I'm late—gotta run. Check in with you soon.

RYAN: Okay. Listen—keep close to Ellie for me. I don't want her getting in over her head. And I don't want any of our overly confident, jackass brokers getting the wrong idea about my sister. I haven't had time to touch base with anyone but you, but as far as anyone in that office with a dick is concerned, she's off-limits.

JACK: Absolutely on the same page there, brother. I'll spread the word. Talk soon.

Day 7 Tues 8/7

"...*N*ot going to happen," Blair mutters into her phone as I'm passing by her office after my chat with Jack's client. "I'm telling you—there's no way to trace it back. I've crossed every T and... Don't be paranoid, Will."

Her door is open a crack, and I can see her leaning against the desk in front of her huge window, her back to the door. She's obviously talking to Lulu's crusty boss, and it's clear from the annoyance in her voice that she's not getting her way.

"Let me worry about that," she says. "You just hold up your end of the deal."

A deal? With Will?

I don't need a spidey sense to know this conversation is not on the up-and-up, but as much as I'm dying to listen in for something that might help Lulu, I can't keep lingering outside Blair's door—not after our run-in outside Ryan's office. She'll think I'm snooping on her.

Which I am. But a girl—even one in disguise—can only handle so much snooping in a single bound. Bringing down the hiring manager from hell will have to wait until I slay a few finance-world dragons.

The rest of the day passes in a crazed frenzy, but I make time to pounce on my leftovers for lunch—day-old drunken noodles are even better than fresh, especially when accompanied by memories of the naughty things that came to pass the first time I relished this meal—and I'm still going strong at five-fifty when an email pops into my inbox.


To: Eric_Webb
   From: Jack_Holt
   Subject: Going to need you to stay late


Hi Eric,

I regret to inform you that I need you to stay late again tonight. I have an issue only you can help me address. Please stop by my office as soon as the floor is empty for the night.


Sincerely,
   Jack


. . .

Fighting a smile, I'm about to craft a flirty reply, but change my mind when I remember the email waiver I signed on my first day as a fake employee. All S&H emails are subject to monitoring, and I'm not giving anyone here a glimpse into our illicit workplace shenanigans.

Those are *my* workplace shenanigans. Mine and Jack's.

So instead, I grab my phone and text.

ELLIE: Might the problem be in your pants, Mr. Holt?

JACK: It's a full body problem, Miss Seyfried. But yes, the pants-area is most definitely involved. How is it you manage to look so goddamned sexy in a beige men's suit?

ELLIE: Maybe you have secret longings you haven't admitted to yourself until now?

JACK: Negative. My longings are all non-secretive and most involve ripping that mustache off your face, pulling those hideous pants down your legs, and devouring your pussy on my desk. I haven't been able to stop thinking about the sexy way you taste, El...

Face going hot, I bite my lip, grateful there's almost no one left to see me blush. Just a couple of stragglers from accounting headed for the door. Even Blair's office is empty —I checked on my way to the bathroom a few minutes ago.

Which means, I'm cleared to head for the executive wing.

And *God*, I can't wait.

Somehow I've managed to get work done today, but it hasn't been easy. Not with half my brain replaying every touch, every kiss, every second of my red-hot evening with my sexy boss. It doesn't help that Jack's wearing a steel gray suit so expertly tailored it hugs every inch of him, from his broad shoulders, to his spectacular backside, to those powerful thighs that were shifting against mine for hours last night.

I now know what it feels like for Jack to urge my legs wider with a flex of one toned quad, and the knowledge has weighed tingly upon me all day. I haven't been able to go more than a minute or two without a zing of sense-memory shivering across my skin. I've been in such a bad way that the first time Jack breezed by my cubicle around noon, I'm pretty sure I drooled.

Luckily, I'd already fetched my noodles from the break room, so there was a reasonable drool-trigger sitting right in front of me.

Now, however, there's no excuse for the way my cheeks heat and my heart races. No excuse for the way I practically dance through empty hallways to Jack's door, my heart in my throat and my breath already coming faster. Just the knowledge that Jack's hands will soon be on my skin is enough to make me dizzy.

And then he opens the door at my light knock, his gaze every bit as hungry as it was when he laid me out on his bed last night and showed me all the sexy, seductive things I've been missing, and the last of my cool evaporates in a puff of lust-colored smoke.

"You summoned me, sir?" I ask.

"Get in here, Eric," Jacks says in a voice that goes straight to my already trembling thighs. "We have something serious to discuss."

"Oh, no. That sounds...serious," I say as I step over the threshold.

"It sure fucking is." A second later, Jack has slammed the door closed and pressed me back against the thick wood, his fingers digging into my waist as his mouth meets mine in a bruising kiss. And even with my Eric mustache still in place, the moment Jack's lips meet mine, I catch fire.

"I've been thinking about this all day," I gasp as I lock my arms around Jack's neck and hold on tight, devouring him.

I am incapable of restraint with this man. I couldn't hide the way he makes me feel if I tried, so I don't bother. I arch closer, rubbing myself shamelessly against him, moaning in appreciation of the steely length swelling behind his fly as he draws us both across the room toward his desk.

"Me, too. How can you get me this hot with that stupid mustache on?" He guides my suit coat over my shoulders, stripping it roughly down my arms before reaching for his own.

"Like I said, maybe you have unexplored desires." My breath rushes out as Jack grips my ass, pulling me tight to where he's so deliciously thick. My arousal spikes hard and fast, making my words husky as I add, "There's no shame in swinging both ways."

"Do you swing both ways, beautiful Ellie?" he asks, his eyes glittering as he reaches for my tie.

I shake my head, mesmerized by the heat in his gaze as he expertly unshackles me from my Windsor knot. "No, I don't, beautiful Jack. I enjoy cock. Especially yours."

"Enjoy," he echoes with a frown, tossing my tie to the floor. "That's a flabby word, Seyfried. I expected something stronger from a grammar enthusiast of your caliber." He slips the top button on my shirt through its hole, making my nipples pull tight beneath the elastic bandages binding them to my chest.

"Relish?" My tongue sweeps out to dampen my lips as he continues to slowly, seductively work open my shirt.

He hums thoughtfully. "Relish is good. *Crave* would be better."

"How about worship?" I'm teasing as I say it, but the word isn't outside the realm of possibility. A couple more nights like the last one, and I'll be on my knees, singing cock-praising hymns and making offerings to the God of Orgasms.

"Worship is excellent. I certainly worship all of..." He trails off as he strips my shirt down my arms, uncovering the bandages binding my chest. Wincing, he runs a finger beneath the tightly stretched fabric "Doesn't this hurt?"

"No. At least, it didn't." I tug at the knot of his tie as I continue in a softer voice, "Until I needed you to touch me. So badly."

"Me, too, El. So bad," he murmurs, popping open the safety pin holding my bandages closed. "I've been dreaming about having you in my mouth all day. Of the taste of your skin and your nipples hard on my tongue."

Before I can confess I've been dreaming about the same thing, he spins me in a circle, lifting me to sit on his desk. A beat later, my bandages are unraveled, and Jack is unraveling me.

The feel of his mouth on my breasts—sucking and biting my nipples until I'm squirming on his desk in anticipation—is even more intense than before. I'm dizzy, reeling, so drunk on his touch, his kiss, that I don't remember when he disposed of my shoes or pants.

I only come back to myself as he squeezes the sock stuffed down my underwear with a sharp huff. "Pretty sure this is the weirdest office sex ever," he says.

"But hot." I reach down to rub his erection through his boxers.

"So hot," he echoes, grinning as he tugs the sock out and tosses it to the floor.

Laughing, I pull him down for another kiss, but soon nothing is funny. Soon, I'm lost, yearning and aching and so desperate for him that the moment he reaches for a condom from his desk drawer, a sob of relief bursts from deep in my chest.

"Oh yes, please." I reach down, helping him roll the latex down his fever-hot length. "Inside me, Jack. Now."

"Yes, Ellie, yes." He drives home with a groan that so perfectly echoes the mixture of bliss and relief coursing through me that it opens the floodgates. As he begins to move, sounds pour from my lips—words and moans and not-at-all restrained cries that fill the air as he takes me there.

*There.*

Oh, God, right *there*, the place where I've only ever been with him, this man who plays my body like a musician who's studied his instrument for years, learning all the secrets that make it sing.

"So good," I gasp, nails digging into the tight muscles of his ass, drawing him closer. "So damn good."

"You make me crazy, El," Jack growls against my mouth as he drives into me harder, faster, building the tension low in my body. "God, baby, I can't wait to feel you come. To feel you lose control on my cock."

I whimper in agreement as I hang on tight, bracing myself for another out-of-body experience. And then Jack slips his hand between our sweating, striving bodies, applying the perfect amount of pressure to my already humming clit, and I'm spinning.

Soaring.

Spiraling.

I come apart, shattering into a thousand glittering shards that catch and reflect and magnify the bliss pulsing through my body until it's almost too much.

Too intense, too sweet, too perfect.

By the time Jack shoves deep, coming with a groan that makes me feel powerful in a way I never dreamt a man's orgasm could—*I* did this to him, *I* made this incredible man fall apart—my throat is tight, and tears are stinging the backs of my eyes.

I wrap my arms around Jack, swallowing hard, fighting to regain control before he notices my emotional meltdown.

But I should know better. Jack doesn't miss a beat.

"What's wrong?" he asks, gently cupping my face. "Fuck, I didn't hurt you, did I?"

I shake my head and force a soft, "No."

"Then what is it?" He brushes his thumb across my bottom lip. "You can talk to me, El. I'm not going to bite."

My lips twitch up at the corners. "Not true."

He smiles. "You know what I mean."

"I know." I blink fast as I lift one shoulder and let it fall. "Nothing's wrong. Everything's good. Too good, I guess. I'm not accustomed to super magical nuclear powered fab-gasms. Caught me off guard."

His grin stretches wider and his chest puffs up, making me laugh.

"Oh man," I say with a sigh. "Your ego just grew three sizes, didn't it?"

"Like the Grinch's heart when he brought back Christmas," Jack says, summoning another giggle from my lips and banishing the last of the tension. "But I'll try not to be too insufferable about it. Though, I would like 'Super Magical Nuclear Powered Fab-Gasm Giver' in my obituary. Could you arrange for that to happen?"

I nod and promise seriously, "Absolutely. Though, I may have to make an anonymous tip to the paper to avoid traumatizing my brother with my dark sex secrets."

Jack's smile dims a watt or two. "Yeah, there is that."

"There is, but we don't have to talk about it." I curse myself for killing the mood with a dumb joke.

"No, we don't," Jack agrees, his eyes narrowing on my upper lip. "What do you say we forget about Ryan and

Eric and work and go grab a drink somewhere fun? Preferably somewhere with a rooftop bar and a killer view?"

"Sounds great," I say. "Except for the Eric part. I have nothing to wear except my suit."

Jacks makes a scoffing sound. "Easily remedied. We go to your place first, then we go out."

My brows lift. "You're willing to come all the way to Queens for me?"

"I'd go a lot farther than Queens, baby," he says, leaning in to press a slow, lingering kiss to my lips. "Can you say the same about Vin Diesel? I think not."

My heart starts beating faster again, but lust isn't the only thing pumping through my bloodstream. There's something sweeter mingled in with the physical longing, something that makes me feel warm from head to toe, even though I'm not wearing a stitch of clothing and Jack's office is always cooler than the rest of the floor.

"Then let's get going," I murmur against his lips. "There's a great Indian place on my block called Masala. Best naan in the five boroughs, and the owner's daughter plays ukulele on Tuesday nights."

Jack pulls away with an arched brow. "Ukulele? And this is a selling point?"

"Don't knock it until you try it," I say, reaching for my shirt. "She's gifted, and she takes requests."

"Oh, well, that's a different story," Jack says, sarcasm thick in his voice.

I smile. "I'm going to ask for *Mother* by Danzig."

He snorts in laughter, making me feel unreasonably proud of myself. I love making him lose control, this man who is usually the master of himself and all he surveys.

"Or maybe some death metal," I add. "Death metal and ukulele are brilliant together."

"I noticed you had a strange record collection." He steps into his pants. "I'll have to take a closer look while you're showering. See just how deep the weirdness runs."

"To the bone, baby," I say, my heart skipping a beat when he laughs and reaches over to affectionately slap my bottom.

"I believe it." He reaches past me for his phone, pressing a kiss to my forehead as he moves. "I'm calling a car. I'm too hungry to take the subway."

"Perfect," I say, that warm-from-inside feeling flooding through me all over again.

It *is* perfect. All of it. From the explosive sex to the sweet forehead kiss to sharing another meal with Jack and everything in between.

If I'm not careful, I'm going to get in way over my head. I shouldn't be fraternizing with one of the CEOs of the firm I'm writing about, especially not when I'm already related to the other CEO. And I certainly shouldn't be starting to fall for him, or daydreaming about this becoming something more than naked fun between two old friends.

Eventually, I'll have to make some tough decisions about this story, and I don't want my judgment to be clouded by complicated feelings, especially when those feelings aren't reciprocated.

Jack is a man of the world. He probably has loads of experience keeping sex and emotion separate. Yes, he cares about me as a friend and his partner's sister, but that's all this is.

Friendship and orgasms...

Right?

I glance over at Jack, who is giving our address to the car service, and he winks, his lips stretching into a smile that's so much more open than the old Jack smile I used to know. Open and so warm I want to wrap it around me and snuggle up with a good book. Preferably a romance novel, something I've been avoiding in recent, lonely years, but which suddenly sounds like fun.

Great, now I'm having snuggle-reading fantasies about Jack to go with all the sex ones.

I'm definitely headed for trouble, but at the moment I can't bring myself to care. Life is a lot more complicated outside my solo-writer, shower-optional lair, but it's also a hell of a lot more fun.

And that's what we have—fun.

From the car ride to Queens, to the quickie in the shower as I get changed, to our long, leisurely, laugh-filled dinner accompanied by the musical stylings of Riya and her Rockin' Ukulele, the evening is pure goodness. It's so good I don't want it to end, but after he walks me back to my place, I let Jack call a car anyway. No matter how much I would like to invite him to stay over, I have to maintain some boundaries. If I don't, I'll have even farther to fall when this is over and Jack and I go back to the way we were.

*Too late. Things are never going back the way they were,* a voice in my head whispers as I kiss Jack goodbye and he slides into the waiting town car.

But it's not the usual voice of doom. It's a voice I

don't recognize, but it's telling the truth. I can feel it in my bones, in my blood, in the warm hum of happiness that follows me up the elevator, down the hall, and sees me tucked into bed with a smile on my face.

And for once, I don't try to talk myself back down to earth with reminders of all the things there are to be afraid of. I stare out the window at the stars fierce enough to be seen above the big city lights and let myself make a wish or two, wondering if Jack might be looking at those same stars right now and doing the same.

# CHAPTER 13

## Jack

Day 8 Weds 8/8

*T*hey say if something *can* go wrong, it probably will.

Never has that old chestnut been more true than today.

The morning started with a slew of technical difficulties during a presentation for a big corporate client, and quickly slid from bad to worse when a major ISP disclosed a global data breach, tanking the Nasdaq. Three of my top guys got waylaid by food poisoning after eating sushi from a place called Captain Bob's Burgers 'N Boat Trash—not sure how they didn't see that coming. And the afternoon closed out with a memo from my systems team that we're due for a tech upgrade next month to the tune of $580,000.

But like its own special brand of pixie dust magic, all

of that bad shit swirls right down the drain when Ellie walks into my office an hour after closing bell.

God, she's stunning. Even in that boxy suit and makeup, she can't hide the real deal from me. Especially not after last night.

Just thinking about all the things we did in this room has me hard and ready again.

"And to think I used to dread late nights at the office." I grin and loosen my tie as she closes the door and crosses to my desk. Beneath the cloying fragrance of Axe body wash—yes, my woman takes her role as a finance dude-bro seriously—I smell the sweet, feminine scent that's all Ellie, and it makes my mouth water. "I missed you like crazy."

I take her into my arms and claim her mouth in a deep kiss, ignoring the tickle of her mustache on my skin.

"Mmm." Ellie sighs against my lips. "Keep kissing me like that, and I might start to believe you."

"If you insist." I lean in for round two, but Ellie puts her hands on my chest, holding me back. Her eyes twinkle with mischief, and I can't keep the grin off my face. "You're killing me, El. You know that, right?"

"I'm trying to be professional, Mr. Holt," she teases. "Which means first we cover work business, then we get to the naughty business."

"Work business? But it's after hours." I'm not sure I can hold out much longer. My hands are already roaming over her curves, sliding under her perfect ass, pulling her toward my rock-hard cock as I give myself a slow-motion mental preview of all the ways I'm going to make her come...

"Five minutes." She squirms out of my grip, tossing her suit coat onto the chair behind her. "I have an update on my research, a quick request, and then I'm all yours. Promise."

"Is the request related to the naughty business?"

She pins me with a no-nonsense look, lips pursed beneath her mustache.

I lift my hands in surrender. "Okay, okay. I'll behave. What've you got for me?"

Ellie perches on the edge of my desk. I sit on my chair in front of her, my hands curled around her hips.

"When it comes to hiring practices and advancement opportunities," she says, "There's clear evidence of preferential treatment toward male employees. It took a bit of time to correlate, but now that all the dots are connected, you can't miss it."

I nod, impressed with her research skills. For the first time since she started this project, I can see the light at the end of the tunnel. The day she turns in her story and resigns from her "position" at S&H is the day we can stop sneaking around and—bonus—the blissful day I stop kissing someone with an intensely tickly mustache. "I'll take your findings to Ryan and Blair, and we can start implementing some changes."

"That's the idea. But..." Ellie exhales with a weary shake of her head. "I'm barely scraping the surface, Jack."

"Hey." I stand, brushing the man-bangs from her eyes. "You're kicking ass. If you need more data, we'll just have to dig deeper. Right?"

She smiles softly. "Thanks for the 'we' part."

"You know I'm all in. So where do we go from here?"

"I have anecdotes from some of the women in the office, but some of these issues are hard to quantify."

"How so?"

"It's not a problem unique to S and H," she says, her voice darkening. "The truth is women are penalized for our biology and our gender roles in almost every facet of life. All the scientific research and the studies I've been reading...it's all so deeply depressing. And if you're a woman of color or an older woman, the roadblocks are even bigger."

I slide my hands to her shoulders, giving her a reassuring squeeze. I hate that I don't have words for this, but I'm out of my depth. As much as it stings to admit it, this past week is the first time I've ever given gender politics much thought.

I've never *had* to think about it before because it doesn't affect me personally.

Kind of proves her whole point...

"It's crazy." Ellie rises from the desk and begins to pace the office. "Most of the time, childcare, healthcare, and other domestic responsibilities fall to women, but women are working outside the home just as much as men. So what happens when a parent has to stay home with a sick kid? Or someone has to take Grandma to the doctor? And what about single parents? Should a mom be punished for leaving the office for a family emergency, even if she's able to make up the work at a later time?" She stops pacing and turns toward me, hands on her hips. "Serious questions, Jack."

I blink as I lean back to sit on the edge of my desk. "I guess it depends on the nature of the job, and what the person's manager—"

"What if the manager is a jerk? Shouldn't there be policies in place to protect employees in this kind of situation? A neurosurgeon can't walk away in the middle of brain surgery, but Seyfried and Holt isn't a hospital. There's no reason why loyal, hardworking employees can't occasionally work from home so they're not forced to choose between their child's health and their ability to put food on the table. Job security shouldn't come down to face-time at the office."

Ellie's cheeks are red, her eyes fiery with emotion that tells me this is much more than an assignment to her. It's a cause. And it's personal.

"I admit we haven't considered anything like that before," I say, "but if we set up ground rules and clarify expectations, I have no problem test-driving that kind of arrangement."

"Maybe *you* don't, but some of your senior managers do. Which is messed up, because studies prove workers are more efficient and productive when they're given trust and flexibility. Which tells me that the managers who vehemently oppose the idea are either control freaks, misogynists, or both."

"I hear you, El. I guess I'm just..." I run a hand through my hair, trying to gather my thoughts. "Why is this the first I'm hearing about this? Your brother and I work hard to cultivate an open-door policy with all of our employees."

Her gaze softens. "But you're not everyone's manager, Jack. Most people aren't comfortable going above their direct supervisors."

I mentally scan through the list of non-executive women on our payroll. Admittedly, I can't even remember most of their faces, let alone name them all. "So none of these women have logged formal complaints?"

"It sounds like there may have been one or two who did so in the past, but I'm told they were let go soon after. I'm still trying to track down the paper trail on that, though—hence my request."

"Okay." It's a lot to process, but I'm ready to tackle this head on, no matter what. "What do you need?"

"Can I get access to the actual personnel database? The printouts were helpful with the hiring issues, but if I want to investigate these other complaints, I'm going to need more data."

"I can set you up with admin access," I tell her. Ryan wouldn't like it—neither would Blair—but we need to get to the bottom of this. "I'll just need you to sign a confidentiality agreement so our bases are covered in case anyone starts digging."

"Of course. And I promise I won't use any identifying information in my article or even in my notes."

"I trust you," I say, surprised at how easily the words come out. But then, everything with Ellie feels so natural, so right, so easy in a way that has nothing to do with how long I've known her family and everything to do with who she is. With how I feel when I'm with her.

"So, anything else on the work front?" I continue, no longer able to hide my smile. I'll stay focused as long as she needs me to, but seeing Ellie all fired up is doing nothing to cool off the situation below my belt.

"That's it," she says. "I just want you to know that I hold myself to the highest ethical standards in journalism."

"I know, El." I push away from my desk.

"And in life."

"No question." I stalk slowly across the room.

"I understand the importance of protecting my sources, and it means a lot to—"

"Ellie?" I stop in front of her, holding her gaze.

Her lips part as she exhales. "Yes?"

"Can we please stop talking?" I pull her back into my arms, nuzzling her neck, just above her starched collar. It's become one of my favorite places to linger, along with the hollow of her throat and the bottom of her ribcage—her most ticklish spot. "Or at least stop talking file access? Because right now all I can think about is how much I want access to your man-pants."

Ellie's laughter transforms into a moan of pleasure as I back her up against the wall behind my desk and slide my hand into her waistband. Despite her steadfast commitment to authenticity, under the uninspiring beige suit she's *all* woman. My fingers skim beneath the lace trim of her lingerie, eagerly seeking her wet heat.

"Have you been thinking up that line...all day?" she asks, digging her fingers into my shoulders as I glide over her clit. I dip a finger inside her, dragging it out slowly before pulsing back in again, loving the way she melts at my touch.

"Longer than that," I admit, kissing her jaw, her ear. Everything about her is silky and delicious. No matter how often I touch and taste her, I can't get enough. "I have a rotating stock. A pun for every occasion."

I slide another finger inside, pumping deeper, my balls aching as her body tightens around me, and holy *fuck* I want inside this glorious woman right now. But she's already close to the edge, and no matter how much my dick throbs for contact, I won't pass up the chance to make her come. To feel her shatter at my touch.

"Yes, I'm right there, Jack. You're...making me..."

"Come." I palm her clit, curling my fingers to hit the perfect spot. Her words are incoherent, her cries of ecstasy so loud I'm sure the janitorial staff must hear us, but I don't care. Right now, all I care about is giving her this pleasure, watching her cheeks turn pink as she rides my hand, her hips bucking, her breath hot and sweet as I capture her mouth in a deep, satisfying kiss.

After the last shudder racks her body, I slowly pull away, and Ellie opens her eyes, gazing up at me in a state of pure bliss. Her lips are swollen, her wig is crooked, and her mustache is curling up on one side like a dead caterpillar, but still she's the most beautiful woman I've ever seen.

I'm about to tell her so when the unmistakable click-clack of heels on the floor in the hallway pops the nirvana bubble.

"Someone's coming," I say.

"Shoot, I didn't lock the door!" Eyes widening, Ellie frantically tries to smooth out her mustache, but it's no use.

"Under here. Hurry." As quickly as I can, I help her duck under the desk, settling myself into the chair seconds before Blair bursts into my office, her face pinched with concern. "Hey, Jack. Is everything okay?"

I inch my chair closer to my desk.

"Why wouldn't it be?" I casually pluck a pen from the holder on my desk as if I'd been looking for it all along. My heart is slamming against my ribs, but on the outside I'm a stone-cold bastard, unruffled by my still-throbbing hard-on, my woman curled up like a cat at my feet, and my hiring manager scanning my office like a PI looking to bust a cheating spouse.

"I thought I heard screaming," Blair says suspiciously.

"What? Oh, must have been that video Ryan sent me." I grab my phone from the desk and shove it into a drawer. "He's hosting a client appreciation party in Portland. Pretty rowdy bunch."

She scowls. "I thought the whole reason he was out there was to *find* clients."

"Exactly. Nothing says 'come on board' like a party." I arch a brow, forcing myself to sit absolutely still as Ellie fidgets beneath the desk. "Blair, you should head home. You work too hard."

"You know I don't mind putting in extra work for the team," she says with a grin. "Actually, I'm looking for Eric. I saw him come this way. Figured he was in here with you. But then I heard the noise and thought maybe you guys were duking it out or something."

Duking it out?

That's one way to put it...

I shrug. "Nope. Haven't seen him. Have a good night, Blair."

Her gaze lasers in on the chair in front my desk with the precision of a military-grade missile launcher. "Is that your jacket?"

About ten sizes too small, but... "Sure is."

She takes another step into the office. "Are you sure you didn't see—"

"Blair? It's been a long day, I still have a few things to

wrap up, and I'd like to get out of here before midnight. If you're looking for Eric, try his workstation or send him an email."

"Right, of course." She glances around the office again. "You're sure you're okay?"

"Good night, Blair." I flash a smile that I hope says "I'm exhausted from a hard day's work" rather than "I have a woman dressed as a man hiding under my desk and you've interrupted what could've been another Super Magical Nuclear Powered Fab-Gasm, and I'd really like to get back to it."

Blair studies me a moment longer, but finally she relents, imploring me not to work too hard before shutting the door and disappearing down the hall.

"All clear, kitten," I tease, reaching under my desk to rub Ellie's ears. "You can crawl back into my lap now."

"Not a chance, Holt. That was too close." She rolls out with a rush of breath. "As of right now, our office sexcapades are officially over. No more desk nookie. Or any other kind of workplace nookie."

"Oh, come on. Where's your sense of adventure?" I grab her hands and try to pull her into my lap, but she's not having it.

"Where's your sense of trying to avoid a lawsuit?"

"Worried Blair is going to sue us?"

"Nothing would surprise me from that woman." Ellie adjusts her wig and her clothes, straightening all the things I worked so hard to un-straighten, before turning to me with a wink, "But lucky for you, one of us has an apartment a few blocks away. With a bed. And no nosy colleagues."

"Hey! That's me!" I vault from my seat, circling the

desk and snatching her suit coat from the chair. "Have I told you how brilliant you are today?"

Her smile widens. "I don't mind hearing it twice."

"Brilliant," I say, tossing her the suit coat. "And sexy. And hopefully fast."

"I'll take the back elevator and be at your front door before you get there," she says, her eyes dancing as she backs toward the door. "Bet you five dollars."

"I'll see your five dollars," I say, "and raise you five orgasms."

Ellie laughs. "I'll hold you to it, high roller."

"Oh, I'm counting on it."

# CHAPTER 14

Day 8 Weds 8/8

JACK: Just checking in. You get home okay?

ELLIE: I'm sorry! I meant to text but got in the bath and lost track of time.

JACK: Are you still in the bath? Naked? Covered with slippery soap bubbles?

ELLIE: Wouldn't you like to know? ;-)

JACK: Yes. Yes, I would. And are you relaxed, Miss Seyfried? Because *I* haven't been able to relax since you left this bed.

ELLIE: Leave 'em wanting more, then reel 'em in—
that's my motto.

JACK: Consider me reeled. Also, I've come to an important decision about one of the great dilemmas of our
time.

ELLIE: Do tell.

JACK: As much as it pains me to say this… You're right.
Office sex is too risky and has to remain off the menu for
the time being.
:-[ (That's my pained face. I am physically pained by the
loss of office banging privileges.)

ELLIE: Hey, don't blame me! Your nosy colleagues are
why we can't have nice things.

JACK: Your screaming orgasms are why we can't have
nice things.

ELLIE: Oh really? Well, maybe I'll have to keep them to
myself from now on.

JACK: Don't even joke. That would be cruel and unusual
punishment. I want your orgasms. All your orgasms.

ELLIE: Oh, well… That might be a problem.
Because I'm working on one right now…
All alone in my bathtub…
And there might be screaming…
I hope the neighbors don't hear…

Oh...
My...

JACK: Stop! Wait! I'm coming over.

ELLIE: Sorry...
Too late. ;-)

JACK: You are evil. Beautiful, sexy, evil.

ELLIE: And you love every minute of it.

JACK: I will neither confirm nor deny my love of your evil.
But back to the office sex situation...
We need a new plan. I can't be expected to go a full eight-hour day without being inside you. It's inhumane.

ELLIE: Agreed. I can't go that long without you, either.

JACK: Elevator? Hit the stop button, tear off our clothes, and go for it?

ELLIE: Cameras. And the alarm would be too distracting.

JACK: True, but great cover for your screaming orgasms.

ELLIE: Good point. :-)
Um...wow. I'm drawing a blank.
Outside? Battery Park on our lunch break?

JACK: We'd probably get arrested. Executive lounge?

ELLIE: No way. Office sex is off the menu, remember?

JACK: Fine. We're just going to have to leave town for the day, find some place where we can get naked in peace.

ELLIE: Montana? Morocco? Mars?

JACK: I was thinking slightly more local. Just far enough away that we won't run into our colleagues. Or *any* people, for that matter.

ELLIE: No people? Now you're speaking my language.

JACK: Perfect. Pick you up at 7 a.m. tomorrow. Plan to be out all day.

ELLIE: Wait... Seriously? What about work?

JACK: This is a sanctioned work event. A corporate retreat. Team-building is an essential part of the onboarding process for new hires, Eric. Didn't you watch the employee orientation video?

ELLIE: Team-building with just two of us?

JACK: I pride myself on giving my staff the highest level of personal attention. And by "my staff" I mean the one between my legs, soon to be between yours.

ELLIE: You really do know how to close the deal, Jack. No wonder you're the boss.

JACK: You ain't seen nothin' yet, baby. ;-) Seven a.m. tomorrow. Bring your fine ass, your mustache-free mouth, and a pair of hiking boots. I'll take care of the rest.

ELLIE: Okay. But you'd better bring some snacks, too, or I won't even make it out of the car.

JACK: As far as I'm concerned, you ARE the snack. But fine...
I'll bring fancy cheese, just for you.

ELLIE: CHEESE! You said the magic word. It's a date. See you soon, sexy.

JACK: Not soon enough.

# CHAPTER 15

## Jack

Day 9 Thursday 8/9

"*S*o what other things around this gorgeous place might be hungry for our blood?" Ellie snags my arm, holding on tight as I sidle up next to her on the primitive hiking trail. "I'm all about the trees, but I'm not good with wild animals, Jack. Especially bears!"

"It wasn't a bear. It was a fisher cat."

"It looked like a bear. A small bear, but a *bear*. No doubt."

"It's more like a weasel, technically. Besides you can't blame the little guy for wanting a bite." I give her a playful smack on her ass—the one that only moments ago was bared to the entire state of New York from the top of a nameless, rarely traversed mountain on the outskirts of the Catskills.

We'd just completed our second "team-building" exercise of the morning—the first happening in the car at the deserted trailhead parking area—when a furball scuttled onto the rocks and screeched like a tiny demon, scaring the hell out of her.

"We could've been attacked," she says, clearly unamused.

"No way. You showed him who's boss with that primal scream of yours. I bet he's already back in his hole, warning his friends about the fierce, five-foot terror of the Catskills."

"Five-foot-*four*, thank you very much." She shudders. "Do you know how many cases of rabies were confirmed last year in New York state alone?"

"How many?"

"I don't remember, but it's a lot. And the treatments are horrible."

She shivers again and tries to speed-walk ahead of me, but I overtake her easily, grabbing her hips and backing her up to a maple tree on the side of the trail.

"Hey. *I've* got teeth and claws and you like to hang out with me." I lean in to nibble her neck, making her laugh as she twines her arms around my neck and kisses me full on.

"How did you even find this place?" she murmurs against my lips.

"Do you like it?"

"God, it's beautiful," she says, eyes wide with appreciation as she takes it all in again. "But it's like the trail that time—and park maintenance—forgot."

"It's always been like this. My parents used to bring

me when I was a kid. Every year or so I find myself grav-
itating back to it. It's not on any of the maps, and most
people stick to the more popular routes, so it's the
perfect getaway."

It *is* perfect. Sunny and clear blue skies, a light
breeze to keep us comfortable, and no one else on the
trail but the forest dwellers. No fretting about stock
valuations, no mind-numbing meetings, and—best of all
—no interruptions.

And I love sharing this place with her.

"Thanks for bringing me," she says. "It's been way
too long since I've stepped on actual dirt and grass
outside a city greenspace."

"I thought you'd enjoy it. Couple years ago, I did a
solo backpacking trip up here—little farther in. No
human contact for ten days."

"Impressive. And it gives me an idea for my next
story." Ellie grins, holding up her hands to frame my
face. "Jack Edward Holt. From Wall Street tycoon to
wilderness wanderer. How does he find the time to be so
consistently fascinating?"

"Admit it." I hook a finger through her belt loop and
tug her close. "You love hanging out with me in the
wild."

Ellie bites her bottom lip, her cheeks pink. "Yeah, I
do. Even with the bears."

"I knew it!" I kiss her forehead. "An adventurer in
the making."

"It was four miles," she says. "Round trip. I'm hardly
scaling Mount Everest."

"You know what they say. 'A journey of a ʻthousand

steps begins with hiking four miles and mounting me on a rocky outcropping.'"

She grins. "I believe *you* mounted *me*."

"To-may-to, to-mah-to."

"You're impossible. Seriously, I—*Jack*!" Ellie gasps as I wrap her up in a tight squeeze, my fingers seeking those ticklish spots along her rib cage.

"Stop!" she squeals, tears of laughter spilling down her cheeks. "Oh my God, Stop! It burns us!"

"Not until you admit that was the most fun you've had since we got high and planned our apocalypse escape. Admit it, Seyfried."

"Okay, okay! You win!" She squirms free and leans back against the tree to catch her breath, still giggling as she tugs a lock of hair from her mouth.

Maybe it's the fresh mountain air, the workout from our hike, or that sexy glow on her skin, but I can't stop staring at her. Can't stop grinning like a kid on Christmas, knowing that I have the power to make this woman laugh like that. That *she* has the power to make this former diehard workaholic bail on his clients so we can play hooky together.

Actually, she has a lot more power than that.

Ellie's the one wearing a mask for this assignment, but I've been doing the same damn thing for more than a decade, hiding behind my confident, master-of-all-I-survey persona.

Ryan is the only person I stayed close to after my parents died—the only one who truly knows anything about my past. Not the headlines version, but the hard, ugly stuff beneath. The crappy year bouncing around foster care. The uphill battle to get my ass into college after my grades dropped in the wake of the accident.

I spent a long time building walls around my heart after that, convinced it was the only way to keep it from imploding again.

But Ellie...

For the first time since the accident, those walls are starting to crumble. She makes me want to open myself up to possibilities. To trust in something good again. To believe, like that happy kid from long ago, that loving someone doesn't automatically come with a one-way ticket to heartbreak.

Yes, we've got great chemistry, the sex is off the charts, and she's so much fun to be with—always has been. But I'd be lying if I said that this is just a good time.

Looking at that smile on her face as we make our way down the last rocky stretch of trail, seeing that sense of adventure peeking out from beneath her practical shell...

Damn. I don't want this thing between us to have an expiration date.

I want to find out where it might lead.

Not just for today, or a few more weeks while she finishes her research, or until Ryan gets back. But...for keeps.

*For keeps.* The thought settles comfortably inside me as if it has been there all along, warm and happy and right. Totally fucking right.

Heading across the deserted parking lot to the car, I see the mountains rising up ahead of us again, and I'm hit with a spark of inspiration so intense it can't be ignored.

It's a great idea. The best idea.

*She has to say yes...*

"Ellie. Have you ever been skiing?

"Once. Ryan took me with a few friends when I was in high school. I got overconfident on the bunny hill and graduated to a blue run way before I was ready. I face-planted into the snow a dozen times before I finally made it down."

"That's it?"

She lifts a shoulder. "I've never been brave enough to try again."

"You need a better teacher."

Her lips curve. "Got anyone in mind?"

"Well now that you mention it, Ms. Seyfried..." I pull her into another embrace, sliding a finger under her chin and tilting her face up.

I know the question I'm about to ask is a big one, for lots of reasons. It's obvious we both feel a connection, but we haven't been hanging out together that long, and we definitely haven't talked about "us"—or what that even means. And if she accepts my offer, we'll probably have to come clean with Ryan.

And then there's the possibility that she'll flat out say no. That the very question will send her running back to the city to wrap up her research, bang out her article, and disappear from my life once again.

But like the beautiful woman in my arms, asking just feels right.

"I have ten days off for Christmas this year," I say, with a hell of a lot more confidence than I feel. Why am

I so damn nervous? "I was planning to hit the slopes in Colorado—do a little skiing, maybe find a few snowshoe trails in Rocky Mountain National Park, get snowed in someplace quiet with a nice big fire. I'd love to take you with me, El."

"Christmas in the Rockies?" Her mouth rounds into a soft, pink *O*, her eyes widening. "Is this... Are you serious?"

I tuck a stray lock of dark brown hair behind her ear, my fingers curling around the back of her neck.

Spending Christmas together, alone in the Rockies... It's not a confession of love or a marriage proposal. Far from it. But it's a big step nevertheless. If I say yes, if I confirm this is, indeed, a real invitation, then we both know I'm inviting her for much more than a mountain getaway.

I'm inviting her into the wild unknown of something more—a future.

"I'm serious," I say, the warm feeling in my chest expanding outward, edging my lips into another grin. "Spend Christmas with me, Ellie. Let me show you one of my *other* favorite places in the world."

She takes a deep breath and lets it out slowly as a grin takes possession of her pretty face. "One question. Will you bring the Cheetos?"

"Baby, I'll bring you whatever you want."

"Okay," she says, still beaming. "Christmas in Colorado. You and me. I'm in."

Her and me. Yeah, that's sounds right.

"We make a great team." I take her hand, dragging her not-so-subtly toward the car. "In fact, I think we should close out this adventure with a post-hike team-building exercise to reinforce everything we've learned today."

Ellie murmurs her agreement, tightening her fingers around mine. "Maybe even two more, just to be sure." Then, gazing up at me with heat and desire and happiness blazing in her eyes, she says, "Because I don't want to forget any of this."

# CHAPTER 16

## Ellie

Day 17 Fri 8/17

*A*fter two weeks undercover, I don't know who I am anymore, and it's not just the cross-dressing or the secret identity that's to blame.

Heck, it's not even *mostly* the cross-dressing or the secret identity.

It's the woman in the mirror, the one grinning her cheeks off as she stuffs her hair under her hideous man-wig and glues fuzz to her face. It's the lightness in my step and the pleasantly full feeling in my chest and the way I was able to talk to my father on the phone for an entire hour last night without feeling like a disappointment to the Seyfried name.

And it's not like my father's lovingly disapproving attitude toward my job or my apartment or the general state of my life has changed. My father is a sixty-five-year-old man who's worked in finance since the Stone Age. He's past the changing age and firmly set in his ways.

Insanely, I'd thought the same thing about myself a few weeks ago—that my future was set.

Variations on a theme—like getting blacklisted from the Barrington Beat if my exposé doesn't hit the right notes, or smoky-eye articles giving way to hard-hitting coverage of another shadow trend—I could envision. But nothing like this.

A complete reversal in course.

A change of the heart.

A revolution of the spirit.

I am no longer a shower-avoidant, lair-dwelling, loner wordsmith. I'm a social creature who leaves my apartment every day, works hard at two jobs I'm enjoying the heck out of—finance on the clock and investigative journalism on the sly—and I'm dating the man of my dreams.

Jack and I *are* dating. We haven't said the words or slapped on labels, but the way he touches me, the way we laugh together, the way we can't keep our hands off of each other no matter where we are or whether or not I'm wearing a fake mustache at the time—all signs point to a swiftly developing relationship.

Maybe even a serious one.

I mean... Christmas together in the Rockies? If that's not boyfriend-girlfriend-level stuff right there, I don't know what is. Since our "retreat" last week, we've been spending even more time together, stealing away to his apartment or mine after work, sneaking in flirty texts or calls, diving deeper into the waters of intimacy than I ever have before. Especially this early in a relationship.

But I'm not scared. Or anxious. I'm just...happy.

Jack makes me happy. I like who I am when I'm with him and who he is when he's with me and how the world looks when his hand is in mine and the taste of him lingers on my lips.

And yes, he also makes me *seriously* horny. Crazy horny. Legendary levels of epic horn-dossity.

The thought inspires a full-body shiver I can't suppress, even though I'm in an elevator full of suits headed back up to the office from lunch. Good—let them think I'm lacking the manliness to suppress displays of bodily weakness. I'm too filled with excitement (and yes, maybe a touch of terror) to care.

As much as I want to dwell only on the positive, there are mountains left to climb before we run away to frolic in the Rockies.

Sooner or later—like, before Christmas—Jack and I are going to have to give this thing a name, come out of the closet, and figure out what to tell my brother—who, there's no doubt in my mind, is *not* going to be happy that Jack and I are hooking up.

I'm almost ashamed of how happy I am, especially considering the fresh dirt I keep uncovering on S&H and how *not great* this company is going to come across in my article if I'm not careful. Which is a shame because there are so many good things happening here, too—great things—and dozens of amazing people doing their best to make responsible and creative financial choices for their clients.

Yes, S&H has flaws and failings, but they're the same

flaws and failings so many companies struggle with. They're all going to experience growing pains, and at least Ryan and Jack are open to evolving.

*Eager* to evolve, in fact.

It's what I keep repeating to myself when I get anxiety sweats while I'm pouring over the detailed database records. Jack and Ryan *want* to know. They want to change.

They want to stop things like the scene unfolding this morning in the far corner of the office.

"Sorry isn't good enough anymore, Ms. Rivera." Will Pool, Lulu's pompous, moldy human potato of an advisor, talks loud enough to ensure the people showering in the gym downstairs can hear him. "If you leave this office again without bringing in a doctor's note for your *deathly* ill son, we're going to have to let you go."

The stricken look on Lulu's face is all the convincing I need to start across the room.

"Please, Mr. Pool," Lulu says in a much softer voice. "My son isn't deathly ill. I told you sir, he—"

"Then why do you keep leaving?" Will cuts in with a condescending sigh. "You say you can't live without this job, and yet you keep making excuses to go home before your work is done."

"They're not excuses, sir." There are tears in Lulu's eyes now, but I can tell she's fighting them with everything in her. "It's my son's school. They have a zero-tolerance policy for—"

"My tolerance is close to zero at this point, as well." Will's upper lip curls into a sneer. "If you leave today without that note, don't bother returning."

"But... I have to pick up my son. He's my *child*. I can't just leave him."

"Of course not." Will nods curtly, as if the matter is settled. "Go ahead and pack up your personal belongings. You'll need to turn in your employee ID card before you leave. Your email and database access will be terminated immediately."

"Are you firing me?" Lulu's voice is shaky, her shoulders sagging with the weight of this awful news.

"Mr. Pool, why don't we take this to a conference room for further discussion," I suggest, coming to stand in front of Lulu, shielding her from some of the prying eyes watching this train wreck unfold. "Preferably with Mr. Holt involved. I've been talking with Lulu about her situation and I—"

"And the last time I checked, Mr. Webb," a sharp voice cuts in, "you're neither Lulu's supervisor nor a member of HR, so I'm not sure what your interest is here."

I turn to see Blair—the human splinter stabbing deep into the tender flesh of my otherwise copacetic new life— coming in fast from my right, inspiring in me the irrational urge to grab Lulu by the hand and make a break for it.

But this kind of trouble isn't something either of us can run from, so I roll my shoulders back and stand my ground.

"No, I'm not part of HR," I admit coolly. "But the Federal Family and Medical Leave Act entitles employees to up to twelve weeks of leave to take care of sick relatives without losing their jobs. Lulu's son has food sensitivity issues that require Occupational Therapy, but due to the demands of her job, she hasn't been able to get him to his appointments."

I glance at Lulu, who nods eagerly, seemingly emboldened by my presence. She's not alone in this, and I refuse to let her or anyone else be bullied and intimidated.

"Yes, Eric's right," Lulu says. "Like I said, Mr. Pool, he's not deathly ill, but Matteo absolutely has a medical condition that needs treatment. That's why I spoke to you a few months ago about working from home on Thursdays. If we could make that happen, I wouldn't need to take leave at all. I could get Matteo to an extra therapy session every week, still get my work done while I'm home with him, and hopefully the problem would be resolved in a few months. I can already see improvement in Matteo's eating, even with just the Saturday morning visit."

Mr. Pool lets out an unimpressed breath as his flat brown eyes shift Blair's way. "Ms. Keneally, you're the expert on federal policies, but when I was coming up, employees were expected to balance work and family without costing the company money and inconveniencing their superiors."

"When you were coming up, women stayed home with the children so men could focus on their careers. Is that what you mean?" I ask, my voice every bit as sharp as Blair's. "Because if it is, then I regret to inform you that the world has changed, and it is the responsibility of employers to—"

"You're out of line, Eric," Blair cuts in, her pale face marked with blotches of red near her cheekbones. "Mr.

Pool and I have discussed Lulu's situation in great detail."

*I bet you have.* I think back to that call I overheard last week—Blair and Will talking about some kind of deal they'd made. It must've been about Lulu.

My gut twists as I try to connect the dots.

Blair continues. "Lulu's repeated absences for alleged family issues is—"

"What's *alleged* about it?" I ask with a huff. "The school calls her to come collect Matteo because he's been sick. That's a verifiable fact."

"As I was trying to say," Blair continues, surveying me with a smug disdain that's even more infuriating than open hostility, "there are factors at play aside from Ms. Rivera's absences. Factors her supervisor and I discussed at length before deciding on a strategy for handling this situation. Lulu's termination is not up for discussion— particularly with you, Mr. Webb."

"I'm sorry, but I don't understand." Lulu lifts her arms, palms to the ceiling with fingers spread wide. "What factors? I've never had a bad performance review and—"

"We can discuss this in my office, Lulu," Blair says. "I, for one, don't believe in airing dirty laundry in public."

*Then I really hope you're not a Barrington Beat reader, because laundry day is coming, sweetheart...*

Blair steps back, motioning for Lulu to precede her.

With one last mournful, but grateful, glance my way, Lulu hurries around the corner and down the hall. Mr. Pool grunts, staring down his nose at me as he thanks Blair for her professionalism—his tone clearly inferring that I am the foil to her competency and class—and then I'm alone with the ambassador for female-enforced misogyny.

More than anything, I want to call Blair on her sins, name every law she's bent or broken with her discriminatory hiring practices, point out all the legitimate employee concerns and complaints she's dismissed or buried, and wipe that self-righteous expression from her face.

Instead, I bite the insides of my cheeks and keep my mouth closed. I can't tip my hand or give her the chance to cover her tracks, not until I've got all the evidence I need and am ready to run with this story.

"Listen up, Eric, because I'm only going to say this once." Blair steps closer, until only a few inches separate her pointy red pumps from my leather dress shoes. "Keep your focus where it belongs—on your work and *your* work only—and we won't have any problems. Pull over into my lane again, however, and I won't hesitate to run you off the road."

I hum in mock thoughtfulness. "Unless you're asking me to do your work for you, right? The way you did on my first day in the office, when you thought I'd be an easy mark?"

Blair's blue eyes narrow into frosty slits. "You don't want to start this with me, Webb. I'm not the kind of enemy you can afford to make. Between your whiplash-inducing fast-tracking and the gaps in your resume, I already have enough red flags to recommend a review of your work history. Keep pushing and I'll put the review wheels in motion, and you can be damned sure I'll find a dismissal-worthy offense." Then, in a voice so low and menacing it makes me shiver, "One way or another, I always do."

I balk at the threat, rocking back on my heels. I haven't been suffering from any delusions about Blair's character, but I hadn't considered she might falsify evidence to get rid of me.

But she would—and evidently *has* in the past. There's no way I'm misinterpreting those last words.

For a moment, I'm too shocked to speak—reeling as I wonder how on earth this woman fooled Jack and Ryan into thinking she was a decent human being.

Blair takes advantage of my silence to drive her point home. "Stay out of my way, and keep your mouth shut about things that don't concern you. Or you'll regret it."

"No, you'll regret it," I say in a quietly hostile voice I barely recognize. "I won't be bullied, Blair. And I won't stop standing up for people you're steamrolling for your own selfish reasons. Get your act together and start treating people with fairness and compassion or you'll be the one sitting in a ditch, wondering how you managed to total your once promising career."

Her cheeks blanch before flushing redder than before. "Fine. We'll play it your way. But don't say I didn't warn you."

Before I can remind her this isn't a game—people's *lives* are hanging in the balance, and Lulu and her family will suffer needless hardship if Blair insists on going through with the firing—she spins on her heel and stomps away. I'm tempted to follow her and eavesdrop on her meeting with Lulu, but that's not going to help the situation. I have to go over her head.

But first I need to make sure I have all my ducks in a row.

People like Blair may be meticulous on the outside when it comes to rules and record-keeping, and they're experts at snowing just about everyone. But journalism has taught me one thing: no matter how good people are at covering their tracks, they always leave a paper trail. A fingerprint. Some shred of evidence ready to blow their cover wide open.

More than sabotaging her female employees with unfair hiring practices, or falsifying reasons for termination, she's up to something nefarious, and she's going to great lengths to throw me off her scent. I can feel it in my bones.

And I'm not going to stop until I expose her dirty secrets.

Sitting down at my desk, I log out of my company email and wait for the blank login screen to appear.

*Seyfried & Holt employee emails may be monitored.*

The words are there in black and white, a reminder on the screen as well as on the waivers every single employee signs upon hiring. I doubt that waiver was put in place for emergency snooping situations like this one —and Jack would almost certainly forbid it—but desperate times call for desperate investigative measures.

Sometimes it's better to ask for forgiveness than permission. Especially if the forgiveness request is accompanied by solid evidence of employee corruption.

I pop Blair's email alias into the login screen. It takes nearly an hour and some trolling through Blair's social media feed for inspiration, but I finally crack her password—KateSpadeAddict1—proving she's not nearly as clever as she thinks she is.

I'm in.

At first glance, her inbox is relatively uninspiring, but then I click over to her trash and things get more interesting. Like, emails from someone at the Department of Justice kind of interesting...

"What are you up to, Blair?" I murmur as I screenshot the email requesting a happy hour date be moved to a bar farther from the financial district, and go looking for more evidence.

I don't have anything solid yet, but I've always had a good reporter's nose and right now it smells something foul.

And where there's stink, there's story.

Even before Lulu is escorted out of the office with a box full of her things and her purse hitched over her shoulder, I'm determined. After seeing her devastated face and the dejected slump of her shoulders, I'm devoted.

Story or no story, I'm going to make this right.

# CHAPTER 17

## Jack

Day 17 Fri 8/17

*L*ike Pavlov's dog, I've come to expect the chime of a text notification at the end of a long day of work, and right on cue tonight, it hits.

And right on cue I'm hard again, imagining all the filthy things I plan to do to my sweet, seductive sex kitten as soon as we're off company property. Her every touch, every smile, every kiss makes the long days worth it. I don't know how this will work after she wraps up her story and is no longer a fixture at S&H, but I have no doubt we will find a way.

Like so many things in life, there are no guarantees. But for the first time in my mine, I've found a risk my heart is willing to take.

The chime dings again, and a smile spreads across my face as I glance down at my messages...

My dick instantly shrivels.

The messages aren't from Ellie. They're from Blair.

*We need to talk. It's urgent.* Followed by, *I'm on my way over.*

Shit.

I text a quick response—*Already heading out for the night*—but before I can tap send, I hear the clip-clop of her heels and then a sharp knock on the door.

I briefly consider hiding under the desk, Ellie-style, but Blair's already letting herself in.

Schooling my features into something slightly less murderous, I nod a terse acknowledgment. "Make it quick, Blair. I have a dinner meeting with Eric, and I'm already running late."

In a small, watery voice that's so unfamiliar I do a double take to check that it's still my tough-as-nails hiring manager standing there, she says, "You may want to cancel that dinner."

"No can do." I have no idea what's going on here, but the last thing I'm interested in is wasting valuable putting-my-mouth-on-Ellie time by playing guess-what's-bothering-me with Blair. "Eric and I need to wrap up our recommendations for the Dunn account by Monday morning, and we've got a lot of ground to cover. So, if you don't mind, I—"

"Actually, Jack, I do mind." She closes her eyes and presses her fingers to her lips. After another beat, she looks at me again and says, "Eric is the reason I'm here."

*Oh, shit. Please don't tell me she found Ellie snooping through the database...*

"Is there a problem?" I ask.

"That's an understatement." Blair closes the door with a laugh that cuts off sharply as her face crumples. She looks a hot second away from bursting into tears.

"What's going on?" I ask.

*Jesus, is she crying?* I've never seen her so emotional. Hell, some of my guys shed tears every time the Dow breaks a record, but I can't recall spotting a single crack in Blair's friendly, all-business facade.

Handing over my box of tissues as Blair settles into the chair in front of my desk, I ask, "Are you all right?"

"No. Not really." She blots her nose, then takes a shuddering breath. "I hate this, Jack. I debated all morning about whether to say anything at all. I'm sure it was a misunderstanding, but... Oh, man, this is so hard!"

"It's okay, Blair. Take a deep breath, then tell me what's going on."

"It's just the more I think about it..." Her throat works as she shakes her head. "I know I can't stay silent."

"Whatever it is, I'm sure we can figure it out." My mind is rapid-firing excuses—*I've got Eric on research duty; he signed an NDA; I'm thinking of making some structural changes and asked him to pull performance files...*

"The thing is," Blair says, "I really don't want to involve legal. I came to you first because I know you're a man of integrity, and if there were ever anything...*untoward* going on, you would know how to handle it."

I sit back in my chair, thrown. "Untoward? About Eric?"

"I was as surprised as you are, believe me." She holds my gaze, shredding the tissue in her hands. "But truly,

Jack, I'm hoping we can handle this quietly. As much as he hurt me, I don't want to make trouble."

"Wait. Eric *hurt* you?" The room is spinning as I try to keep up with Blair's story. None of this makes any sense. Could she be mistaking someone else for Eric?

"He..." Blair touches the ragged tissue to her nose again. "Last night, I came back to finish up some work, and he was... He was waiting for me in my office."

My jaw clenches tight. "All right. And what happened then?"

She meets my eyes across the desk, tears streaming down her cheeks. I ball my hands into fists, trying my damn hardest to brace myself for whatever bomb she's about to drop.

"He asked me to shut the door. I was a little thrown, but I wasn't really *alarmed*, so I did it. I assumed he had an HR issue to address—we'd been talking about some of the gaps in his qualifications, so I thought maybe he wanted to revisit that."

"But that's not what happened."

"No, he... I..." She clears her throat, then smooths her skirt, her eyes still glassy with emotion.

I don't know whether to comfort her, to call someone else in here, or to call Eric to come explain this away, because Eric is *Ellie* and Ellie would *never* do anything to upset anyone like this. She's passionate, not cruel, for God's sake...

I'm at a loss for actionable steps, but I know without a doubt that whatever comes out of Blair's mouth next is going to be a serious fucking blow. I can sense it, like the crackle of electricity in the air before a storm, or the hum of energy on the trading floor in the moments before the opening bell.

"Eric...exposed himself to me, Jack."

"Exposed what?" I blurt out.

The mustache glue? The elastic bandages holding the curves in place? Her whole undercover story and the borderline questionable lengths she's gone to in order to get her scoop?

What on earth could Ellie have done?

Lowering her gaze, Blair drops the final bombshell. "His penis, Jack. He exposed his penis."

# CHAPTER 18
## Ellie

Day 17 Fri 8/17

The text comes through a little after six—but I'm so far down the email rabbit hole of Blair's DOJ convos, I don't realize something's off until I rip my gaze away from the screen long enough to read—*Leave quietly and meet me at the Hideaway in thirty minutes. Make sure no one sees you walking out. Especially Blair. But if you do run into her, don't say anything. Not a word.*

With a combination of irritation and concern, I text back—*If she's been telling tales about "Eric" I can explain. We had words this morning, but I stand by what I said. You will, too, once you hear my side of the story. She was out of line.*

"And possibly out of her mind," I mumble, rubbing my eyes with my finger and thumb.

A person would have to be out of her mind to betray a company that had treated her so well, right? But the more I dig, the more it looks like Blair's done just that. Her cryptic emails to and from her contact at the Department of Justice are so bizarre they're practically written in code, but one thing is certain: there's money involved. Lots of it.

And Blair seems to be going to great lengths to hide it.

After what seems like an unreasonably long pause, a few terse sentences pop through on my cell—*Can't talk now. Meet you at the bar. Don't order a drink until I get there.*

I shake my head with a huff. I'm tempted to text back some terse words of my own insisting I can handle a beer and a grown-up conversation at the same time, but I resist. I'm sure Blair made her side of the story convincing, but Jack was my friend long before he was my lover. As soon as he hears the truth, he'll be back on my side.

Or so I assume.

I'm so naïve that I truly assume everything's going to be okay, right up until the moment Jack settles onto a stool beside me at the Hideaway, looking exhausted, but as handsome as ever, and announces that it's over.

"What's over?" I ask, my throat going so tight the words emerge as a wheeze.

He can't mean... There's been no sign, no warning. Everything has been so damned good. Great. Incredible.

Hasn't it?

"Eric," he says, the word inspiring knee-buckling relief and confusion in equal measure. "No more Eric, no more investigation, no more story."

"But I'm so close to—"

"It's too late, Ellie." The tension in his voice makes it

clear how close he is to the edge. "We're on the verge of being found out, and if that happens, it's not just your story that's screwed. Our relationships with Ryan, my rapport with my employees, the trust I've worked so hard to build with my clients, it's all on the line. If word gets out that I aided and abetted an investigative journalist poking around my own company, I'm finished." He lifts his hand to summon the shaggy-haired bartender manning the only hole in the wall left in the financial district.

Because apparently Jack's *that* worried about being seen with me.

Or rather, with Eric.

"Two scotch on the rocks," he tells the man. "The best you've got."

"So much for staying sober," I grumble.

"Jesus, Ellie. We should've quit while we were ahead."

"But why?" I ask. Telling Jack I prefer whiskey can wait. "Because Blair is sick of me standing up for the little guy? If that's the case, you're making a mistake. Lulu Rivera is in the right, and if she decides to litigate, it's going to be—"

"Lulu?" Jack's brows snap together. "What about Lulu?"

I'm shocked that he doesn't know. "Mr. Pool fired her, and Blair backed him up. Lulu was marched out like a criminal this afternoon, let go for the sin of going to pick up her sick kid one time too many. I can't believe Blair didn't tell you. Isn't she supposed to report all personnel changes to you and Ryan?"

Jack curses as he drags a clawed hand through his

hair. "She didn't get around to it. She was too busy giving me an earful of bullshit."

I shake my head. "About what? Talk to me, Jack. Let me help you fix this."

"You can't fix it."

I swallow the ball of nerves in my throat. Does she know I've been poking around her emails?

No matter. She won't have a leg to stand on once Jack knows the whole story.

"Jack, whatever this is—"

"It's... I'm just gonna say it." He leans in, adding in a softer voice, "Blair's claiming Eric exposed himself to her last night."

A cry of outrage leaps from my throat, but Jack presses on.

"The only way to prove she's a lying, scheming bitch is to come clean about your story." He closes his eyes, pinching the bridge of his nose. "Which is not an option. So we're left with this: Eric resigns quietly and disappears, and I figure out how to get rid of Blair without a lawsuit."

"Are you crazy? Then she wins!" My hand balls into a fist on the bar next to the glass of scotch the bartender just delivered. "What if I really were a man facing this accusation? Is that how you would handle this? Get rid of me without proof or an inquiry or even a chance to tell my side?"

"Of course not, but you're not a real man." Jack's breath rushes out as he reaches for his drink. "And if you were, I'm not sure how we would handle it. Blair's been with the company for years; you're brand new and coming to us with some holes in your resume..." He takes a drink, humming around the mouthful of scotch before he swallows. "Honestly, if I didn't know for a fact that you don't have a dick to flash, I would've believed Blair. And I would've found a way to dismiss Eric without making any more waves."

I grip my glass tight, squinting up at him in the darkness. "But that's bullshit, Jack. And not fair to anyone. If some guy really had exposed himself to Blair, she would deserve justice. And the creeper who whipped it out would deserve to have the incident follow him to his next job interview, so the people there know what kind of person they were dealing with." I lay a hand on my bound chest. "And if Eric were falsely accused, he would deserve justice, too. Which would include a chance to defend his reputation and his livelihood. Don't you see?" I stab my finger onto the bar between us. "This proves the entire point of my article. Gender inequality is bad for everyone—women *and* men. It creates a toxic environment where no one is treated fairly and—"

"I'm on your side, okay?" Jack cuts in with a sharp exhale. "Please, Ellie, just give me a break for once. I understand where you're coming from, but this situation is outside all the usual boxes. You're a cross-dressing undercover reporter, and Blair is a sociopath who's somehow managed to fool our entire office for years."

"She isn't fooling everyone," I grumble. "Especially people who don't have a dick."

Jack's eyes lift to the ceiling. "Not everything is boys versus girls, El."

"But this is," I insist, the taste of betrayal sour and miserable in my mouth. "And I can't believe you don't see it. I can't believe you're telling me to give up and disappear without a fight." I slide off my stool, pushing my untouched scotch toward him. "I've got to go. I promised Sonia I would watch Project Runway with her tonight."

"I'll come with you." Jack tugs his wallet out of his pants. "We're not done discussing this."

"Yes, we are," I say, the back of my nose stinging. "I'm not going to tuck tail and run because Blair told a flashy lie. I'm not built that way."

"Ellie, please. I know you're passionate and committed to this, and I respect the hell out of you for that, but—"

"Do you?" I press my lips together, fighting to maintain control. "Because it sure doesn't feel like it. It feels like you're ready to pull the rug out from under me the second things stop being easy."

Hurt flashes in Jack's eyes. "That's not fair. I'm in a dive bar having a lover's quarrel with another man in public for you, El. The entire bar has been staring since we walked in, but I don't care."

I glance over my shoulder, causing the three burly guys at the end of the bar to shift their attention quickly back to their beers and pretend they aren't hanging on our every word.

I turn back to Jack, swallowing hard. "This isn't a lover's quarrel. This is you telling me to ditch a project that could help your employees and re-launch my career. This is you deciding that covering your own ass is more important than doing what's right." I swallow hard, but I can't stop the truth from emerging softly into the air. "That it's more important than me."

"That's not even close to true." Jack's expression

morphs from hurt to flat-out wounded. "You're important to me, Ellie. So fucking important. I thought I
made that clear. These weeks with you... They've been
amazing."

"I thought so, too. But now you're—"

"You have to know what you mean to me. This Blair
situation has nothing to do with the way I feel about
you. The way I feel about us."

I sniff, but I'm losing the battle against a breakdown.
It's time to get out of here. Now. Ten minutes ago. "I'm
not sure about us, Jack. I'm not sure about anything
right now except that I need to see this story through,
and I hope to God you'll let me."

Jack calls for me to wait, but I'm halfway to the door
and I keep going. I lunge out onto the street, squinting
in the suddenly too-bright light as I hurry around the
corner and make a break for the subway entrance at the
end of the block. I don't pause or look back until I'm
three steps down the stairs leading to the platform.

But when I do, Jack is nowhere to be found.

He let me go.

Without a fight.

It doesn't bode well for the future of my article or
my future with this man who is quickly becoming such a
big part of my life.

The best part.

Or so I thought. But maybe I was fooling myself
about that, too. All I know for certain is that I can't
remember the last time I felt this low, so far down that
even the urine stink on the subway platform makes me
ache for Jack and all the dreams I might have to leave
behind.

# CHAPTER 19

## Jack

Day 20 Mon 8/20

y Monday morning, my email inbox is a war zone, each message a grenade lobbed straight into my lap by Blair fucking Keneally.

Subject: Eric Webb

Subject: Next steps with Eric

Subject: Eric's transition off the team

Subject: We need to deal with this expediently

ALL WEEKEND I walked around in a haze of anger and denial, trying to convince myself this was just a bad dream. That I'd wake up this morning relaxed and refreshed, Ellie murmuring in my arms, the sun beaming through my windows to bleach away this Blair-induced nightmare.

But of course, it wasn't a dream. And Ellie's been avoiding my calls since our argument at the bar Friday, dodging me at every turn. "Eric" hasn't even shown up for work today.

She's spooked, which I get. But she's also pissed at me, which I don't get. I'm one hundred percent in her corner on this. Can't she see that I'm only trying to protect her?

Though I know it's probably futile, I pick up my phone and send Ellie yet another text. *You okay?*

She doesn't respond, so I try again. *I'm sorry this is happening. I don't know what the right thing is here, El, but I'm confident we'll figure it out together. I need you to trust me on this. Please?*

Still nothing. Damn it. I know I didn't handle things all that well the other night, but she's got to know she can count on me. With this or anything else.

*Can we meet for lunch today?* I try. *Talk this out?*

I wait ten more minutes, but my phone is dead silent.

My email? Well, that's another story. Two more from Blair, less than a minute apart.

SUBJECT: WHERE ARE YOU?

. . .

AND FINALLY, the one that obliterates the last of my hope—

SUBJECT: Confirmed - meeting with legal

SHE'S NOT LETTING this go. In fact, it seems she's prepared to double down on the whole bullshit harassment story, all to get Eric out of the way.

I've known from the start that Blair didn't like that I hired Eric without her input, and sure, maybe the two of them butted heads a few times.

But why would Blair do something so extreme?

I'm about to pick up the phone and call her *and* Ellie on a conference call so we can put an end to this charade once and for all.

But then Hannah buzzes me on the intercom.

"Ryan is on line one for you," she announces. "He says you're not answering your cell. Everything okay?"

"Not especially," I say, more to myself than Hannah.

"Should I take a message?"

"No, put him through."

I've dodged Ryan—and this entire situation—long enough. I need to give him a heads up about Blair, let him know I'm on top of it before he hears it from someone else and blows this whole thing out of proportion.

"Hey, Ryan." I force a smile, hoping my bullshit cheer shines through to the other end of the line.

"Care to explain why the hell Blair Keneally called me this morning, threatening to sue?"

So much for cheer.

I drop my head into my hand. "I was hoping to tell you about it myself. I'm still gathering all the pertinent info."

"Dude, she told me your new broker-boy flashed his junk, and you didn't even believe her. Newsflash, Jack. When women come forward like this, we fucking believe them."

"Goes without saying." In fact, if Blair had accused any other guy in this office—any *actual* guy—I'd have believed her first, and asked questions later. But Blair isn't a woman coming forward. She's a woman trying to sabotage another woman for reasons I've yet to uncover.

"Then what did you say to get her all riled up?" Ryan asks.

"Just that she was making serious allegations, and as such, we needed to follow the appropriate protocol, which doesn't include firing someone without an investigation."

"Screw protocol. We can't have this kind of shit going on in our company, Jack. No way."

"But Eric doesn't even have—" A dick, I almost say, but catch myself just in time. "He doesn't have access to her office."

Not to mention the fact that at the time of the alleged exposure, "Eric" was busy getting soaped up in my shower after a rowdy after-work romp that may or may not have involved maple syrup.

"Clearly, he does," Ryan says.

"I'm telling you, Ryan. She's lying."

Ryan lets out a frustrated breath. "Why the fuck would she do that?"

"I'd like to know the answer to that myself."

"Jesus, Jack." Ryan hesitates; I can almost hear the damn wheels turning in his head. Then he says, "All right. Suspend the guy, pending investigation. That's protocol. Then let legal do their thing. If the allegations are true, he's out on his ass. Probably even facing charges." Ryan sighs. "Look. I know I've been reluctant to admit we have problems in the office, but sexual harassment? That's a zero-tolerance offense in my book."

"We're in agreement there."

"What's this Webb guy's deal, anyway?" Ryan asks. "Blair says you vouched for him. Brought him in outside the usual channels."

Technically Ryan brought "him" in the day he volunteered me to keep an eye on his sister, but no need to split hairs.

"Eric is not the bad guy here," I say, keeping my voice measured. "Blair is up to something. I just need time to prove it."

"Blair has been an excellent employee from the start. Opportunistic, sure. A little on the manipulative side. But I can't see her lying about something like this."

"You've been gone a while."

"Three weeks is hardly a while, Jack."

I shake my head. Isn't it, though?

Three weeks ago, Ellie was my best friend's little sister. A woman I crushed on from a distance, then did my best to avoid.

But somehow, between her first interview in that horrid fake 'stache and now, I've been swept up in her irresistible tide. I let my guard down.

I fell in love with her.

The realization hits me all at once, a sucker punch to the gut that nearly knocks the wind out of me.

I'm in love with Ellie Seyfried. With the sound of her laugh. With the way she closes her eyes and hums when she drinks strong coffee. With her singular devotion to cheese. With the way her brain works when she's figuring out a tough research problem and the way she feels in my arms when I hold her close and the way she makes me want to be a better man.

For her.

Because a woman with Ellie's heart and integrity and bone-deep commitment to making the world a kinder place deserves the best. I love watching her break through her own boundaries, and love standing beside her while she stands up for what she believes in.

Who she is, who she's still becoming—they both inspire the hell out of me. I want in with Ellie, one hundred percent. I want to be there for every step of the adventure, no matter how hard things get. Now. Tomorrow. Always.

But thanks to my epic fumble Friday night, I'm not sure I'll get that chance.

"I still don't see Blair's angle," Ryan says, dragging me back to craptastic reality. "Odds are she's telling the truth. Women don't usually lie about this shit."

"Well, this one is," I say. After spending the better part of three weeks between Ellie's thighs, or anticipating the *next* time I'd be between her thighs, or dreaming about the *last* time I'd been between her thighs, I'm pretty fucking certain "Eric Webb" is biologically incapable of exposing a dick to Blair or anyone else.

Not that I'm suicidal enough to share that tidbit with Ryan.

"I don't have time for this," Ryan continues. "Rictor and I are *this* close to locking down the Ian Fox account, and word is he's got a couple of other guys from the team interested in what we have to say."

"I know it's bad timing—"

"Bad timing? No. Bad timing is when you come home a day early for spring break and walk in on your Dad banging his girlfriend on your favorite Star Wars sheets."

"Dude." I crack a smile, despite my dour mood. Ryan's crazy. I love him like a brother, but hell, that boy needs some serious help. "Have you ever considered therapy? Just throwing it out there."

"This isn't funny, dickhead. A lawsuit will bring our whole operation down. And if she brings this to the media? It doesn't matter if it's true or not. We'll be crucified."

He's got me there. But of course, I know it won't go that far.

Everything in me is screaming to tell him the truth— all of it. Ellie's his sister, I'm his best friend and business partner, we all want what's best for S&H.

And we all want what's best for Ellie.

He'll understand, right? Eventually?

I take a breath, open my mouth to confess. But...

No. I can't do that to Ellie. I promised I'd keep this secret. Telling Ryan now would mean betraying the woman I love, and I can't do that. Not even to save my own ass from Ryan's wrath—or the media's.

"I'm handling it," I say. "Focus on the Portland office

stuff, and by the time you're back on the East Coast, this mess will be a distant memory."

I hang up with Ryan, my gut tied in knots. Blair's email trigger-finger seems to have calmed down for the moment, but there's a new one from a member of my senior legal staff.

To: Jack_Holt

From: Macy_Parkridge

Subject: Harassment allegations

Jack —

Blair Keneally has looped me in on the situation with Eric Webb. My understanding is that she is not interested in pursuing legal action at this time, however, we are taking her accusations seriously and have assured her that we will investigate and come to a resolution as quickly as possible. To that end, I would like to meet with Eric Webb's immediate team, as well as any assistants or other support staff he may have worked with during his tenure. I've asked Hannah to schedule a mandatory meeting with those individuals, including yourself, for 9:00 AM tomorrow. We'll do a quick general debrief with the group, then arrange to interview them one-on-one. If you'd like to discuss further, please contact me no later than 3:00 PM today.

—Macy

This is bad. *Really* bad.

My job is on the line, my reputation, my relationship with Ryan and every last one of my employees—hell, I could lose everything I've dreamed about and worked hard for since Ryan and I started this place with no more than our MBAs, a little start-up capital, and two big hard-ons for finance.

For so long, it's been the most important thing in my life.

Most people would say I'm crazy to risk it all for a woman.

But Ellie Seyfried has changed everything for me. *She's* what's most important now. I don't care how fast it happened, or what Ryan thinks about it, or what kind of stunts Blair is ready to pull.

Losing Ellie is simply not an option.

But we've only got one choice right now. I just have to make her see that, too.

I pick up the phone and dial Ellie's cell.

She sends me straight to voice mail.

*Damn.*

"Ellie, it's me. Listen. Legal's involved now, and they've set up a meeting for tomorrow morning to interview your entire team. It's only going to escalate from here. I hate that it's come down to this, but we're out of options. We need to come clean. I can break the news, or you can do it yourself, or we can do it together. Your choice, but it has to be done before this meeting tomorrow. We can't let this nonsense with Blair continue. Please call me back as soon as you get this so we can strategize. I'm really worried about you. I'm... Yeah. Call me back. Please."

But she doesn't call back. Not for this voice mail, or the four others I leave throughout the day.

By closing bell, I'm against the ropes—we both are. As much as I hate to move forward on this without her, she's left me no choice.

This ends now.

I start a new email, cc'ing everyone involved.

Subject: The allegations are false. Eric Webb is not a man.

# CHAPTER 20

## Ellie

Day 21 Tues Aug 21

*I*'m ready. Or as ready as I'll ever be.

I'm wearing a new navy designer shift dress I couldn't afford to splurge on, flesh-toned pumps, and a vintage pearl necklace that once belonged to my mother. My hair is swept into an elegant up-do, and Spencer came over early to do my makeup so my blue eyes are popping amidst perfectly blended copper and brown eye shadow and my complexion appears deceptively flawless.

It's been a long time since I've been this well pulled-together, but I might as well be naked.

I feel naked.

Exposed.

Vulnerable and defenseless without my bulky suit and oversize shoes, without my mustache and penciled-in man-brows and the armor that allowed Eric to stride confidently into the S&H offices for three weeks, certain he could make the world—or at least this company—a better place.

I can't believe it's only been three weeks.

I can't believe everything's gone to shit in a weekend.

I can't believe I'm teetering down the hall to the conference room as myself, as Ellie, the compromised reporter and Failure at All Things.

The email from my editor at Barrington came through while I was on the train. An exposé is only an exposé if the reporter isn't outed in the middle of getting her story. Denise no longer has any interest in the piece on S&H, and I doubt she'll want anything else from me in the future.

People say you can't read tone from an email, but Denise is a professional word wrangler. Her five clipped sentences made it abundantly clear that she isn't impressed.

Neither am I.

And neither are the angry, shocked, and betrayed faces that turn my way as Hannah spies me through the windows of the conference room and rises to open the door.

As I step into the charged space, I'm keenly aware of Jack standing in the corner of the room—the smell of him, the tension rolling off his powerful form, the way something deep in my chest aches to turn to him, run to him, wrap my arms around him and hold on tight until we find a way out of this mess—but I avoid making eye contact.

I can't look at Jack, or I won't be able to hold it together through what comes next.

I set my briefcase on the smooth glass at the head of the table, but I don't sit down. Sitting will only make me feel more vulnerable, and I get the sense I won't be here long.

These people don't look like the friends and coworkers Eric knew. They don't look like people who want to ask questions, listen, and come to an understanding. They look pissed off, scared, or too stunned to have an opinion, and I wish all over again that Jack had waited. That he'd trusted me, believed in me, and given me just a little more time.

Or that I had listened to his voice mails sooner, instead of shutting down communication and hiding in my lair like the old, socially dysfunctional Ellie because the thought of losing Jack and this story at the same time was enough to short circuit my coping mechanisms.

I understand why Jack felt backed into a corner, but did he really have to send out that group email last night, before we'd even had a chance to regroup?

If he had waited just a day or two, I might have been able to walk in here with my head held high, a criminal-activity-exposing hero. At the very least, I would've been armed with complete and professionally presented research that would have justified my deception.

But the notes and pie charts I cobbled together after finally listening to Jack's frantic voice mails last night aren't impressive.

As I pull the copies from my briefcase, my hands are trembling. Around two this morning, when it became clear I was going to need every second I could get to pull my presentation together, I emailed Jack, giving him permission to start the meeting before my arrival. I was hoping he would soften them up with the signature Holt charm, and then I'd win them over by explaining why my investigation was so important and dispensing evidence of my solid research skills.

But as I stare at the sea of angry, confused faces, my confidence in my plan crumbles faster than the stale muffin I forced down on my way to the train.

"Before we start looking over the numbers and statistics," I say, my voice thin in the too-silent room, "I want to assure all of you that I never intended to make anyone feel foolish. I truly had, and *still* have, the best of intentions."

"I don't care about your intentions." Rictor's bark breaks the seal on the room, inspiring a chorus of angry grumbles from where the brokers are gathered. "I want to know if your undercover stunt is going to sink the company we've busted our asses to build."

"It's not fair," Frame pipes up, dark eyes wide in his pale face. "A lot of us have families, people depending on us. Making S and H look bad in the media isn't going to make the world a better place for women. It's going to take food off the table for our wives and kids. And do you have any idea how much diapers cost?"

"And childcare," Barb from accounting pipes up.

"I understand where you're coming from." My gaze shifts between Frame and Barb, willing them to see that my heart is in the right place. "This isn't about throwing S and H—or any of you—to the wolves. Through my investigation—"

"Through your deception, you mean." This from

Lulu's supervisor, Will Pool, who isn't even trying to wipe the smear of smug satisfaction from his face.

Plowing on, I say, "I'd hoped to get an insider's perspective and a clearer picture of where a typical financial institution is failing to provide equal opportunity and compensation, and by bringing that to light, start a conversation that might lead to change. Not just here, but—"

"*Might* is the operative word, Ms. Seyfried." Penelope, one of the most senior members of the executive support staff, is clearly unimpressed. "I've been in this game a long time, and change, when it comes, comes slowly. Half the time the people who blow the whistle are tossed out or paid off, the unpleasant things they've exposed are swept under the rug, and the only result is ruined reputations, lost money, and energy, which should be spent getting work done, wasted cleaning up a pointless mess."

"Not all the time. Sometimes policies change and things get better," Wallace says, surprising me. He was kind to Eric, but I wouldn't have pegged him as an ally. "I just hate knowing I was part of an experiment without my knowledge." He blows out a breath, cutting his gaze to Jack. "And I can't believe the execs went along with it."

"That's why I'm here to assure you all that we're going to make this right." Jack steps forward to stand beside me. "Ellie's research was unconventional, yes, but it was also invaluable in pinpointing places where S and H can improve best practices. In the coming weeks, Ryan and I will be reviewing all of Ellie's findings, meeting with any employees who wish to discuss issues and ideas, and implementing positive changes based on your direct input. I'm sorry I misled you, but I will do everything in my power to earn back your trust, if you'll let me."

Wallace nods, and most of the others in the room follow suit. How could they not? Jack is a force. He's not afraid to apologize or admit when he's wrong, and no matter how shaken they were by the news that he's been involved in my research, he's always had their backs.

I just wish he had mine, too.

I lower my eyes, blinking back tears as Jack continues to rally the troops with his detailed plans for making S&H a truly great place to work.

"To that end," he continues, "we're starting immediately with some modifications to our sexual harassment policy and protocols." Jack motions toward the door, where Hannah is seated in her usual chair against the wall, taking notes. "Hannah, if you'll hand out the materials, please? I want to be sure everyone knows the proper channels for lodging a complaint and how that complaint will be evaluated and addressed. We'll walk through the new procedures, then open the floor up for any questions. Sound good?" At everyone's murmurs of agreement, Jack turns to me with a smile that feels forced and thin. "Thanks for coming in today, Miss Seyfried."

And just like that, I'm dismissed.

Jack doesn't tell me to leave, but it's clear that I'm no longer needed—or wanted—here.

Tucking my untouched handouts back into my briefcase, I take a step toward the door, but Jack appears in front of me, blocking the exit.

"Don't go," he says, his voice low. "Stay. See what Ryan and I came up with last night. I think you'll be proud of the changes we're making—all because of you."

Pressing my lips together, I shake my head. "They don't want me here."

"They're just surprised—they need some time to process. Besides, *I* want you here, and I'm the boss."

The cautious smile curving his lips and the hope in his eyes offer the opportunity to salvage at least one beautiful thing from the wreckage of my failed experiment. Jack still wants me. I could stay, suffer through the rest of this uncomfortable meeting, and then go to lunch with my boyfriend.

But as much as a part of me wants that—to be Jack's girl, to be in Jack's arms and his good graces and his bed—the sting of his rejection hurts too damned much.

He didn't reject Ellie the woman he's sleeping with, but his insistence on exposing our plans before I could finish my work set off a bomb in the middle of Ellie the reporter's life.

Ellie the sister isn't faring too well, either.

The message Ryan left on my cell last night was the angriest I've heard my brother since I played bomber pilot with his model airplanes when we were kids, gleefully sailing each wooden masterpiece off the roof to crash onto the driveway below, my five-year-old brain not realizing how impossible it would be to put them back together.

And now Jack and I are the same.

Shattered. Broken.

He made that clear in his response to my email last night, when he insisted this was the only option—we had to tie up loose ends and put everyone's minds at ease before the situation escalated—and revoked my remote access to the S&H systems.

Right. I'm sure everyone's mind is at ease now—especially Blair's, considering I can't get back into her emails and I have no clear evidence to prove she's at the core of something rotten, eating this company from the inside out.

And my hunches? They're not worth much at Seyfried & Holt these days.

So instead of staying and seeing if I can squeeze myself into this new, smaller slice of Jack's life, I shake my head and send a silent farewell to everything we could have been. "I'm sorry. I have to go."

His gaze sweeps my face, his green eyes flickering with hurt. "Are you *leaving* leaving? Or just leaving the office?"

He waits a beat, letting the meaning of his words sink in. Part of me appreciates that he's giving me the choice, but the other part—the softer, more insecure, and much *larger* part—resents him for putting this decision on me. I know the timing sucks—he needs to take care of his employees and do some serious damage control with Ryan right now—but after everything we've been through these past few weeks...

I guess I'd hoped he could do better than "Are you *leaving* leaving?"

Where's the man who taught me how to walk tall and strong? The man who swept me into his arms, wiped away my tears, and made wild, shameless love to me? The man who dragged me up the side of a mountain and invited me to Colorado, his eyes glittering with a thousand unspoken promises of all the things still to come?

Maybe he never really existed at all.

Maybe, like so many things in my life, I completely misread the entire thing.

Telling myself it's for the best, I square my shoulders, and I let him off the hook. "I appreciate everything you've done for me, and I wish you all the best, Jack—truly. But we both know this wouldn't have worked."

It's a lousy excuse, but it's all I've got left.

Jack's brow furrows and his lips part, but before he can respond, Hannah taps him on the shoulder. "Materials are out, boss. Do you want me to pull up the slide presentation?"

As Jack turns to answer her, I slip around him and out the door, breath rushing out in a sigh that is equal parts relief and misery.

I'm grateful the confrontation is over, but knowing that I'll never touch Jack again hurts like someone's carved out part of my heart, leaving just enough behind to register how lonely I'm going to be without him. Before my time with Jack, I hadn't realized how much I craved this kind of connection, how much I ached to be loved and accepted and told that I'm beautiful by a man who means every word.

But now I know, and I can't ever un-know it.

Pressing a fist to my chest, I swear I can feel something sucking away at me from the inside, a black hole of pain where hope used to live.

The thought of going home to my apartment and seeing the bed where Jack and I made love and the floor where we danced and the kitchen table where he sat as I made him my favorite gourmet grilled cheese is unbearable.

No, I can't go home. Not yet.

But I can't go to one of my old coffee shop work haunts, either.

I don't have anything to work on. My story was ripped away just as it was starting to confess its secrets, just as the dots were connecting. I'm not mentally ready to let this go, but I can't approach Jack or Ryan with a gut feeling and a few odd emails, not when they've made it clear they don't want me sticking my nose in S & H's databases.

I have no choice but to move on.

Right?

"Wrong," I mutter, ducking my head to avoid making eye contact with the receptionist at the front desk. I can't handle any more judgy faces this morning.

But I *can* handle this story. I may not be the best at making friends and influencing people, but I'm an animal when it comes to amassing data and reading between the lines. There's something big going down at S & H and I'm not going to let a little resistance—or a lot of resistance—stand in the way of making sure Blair faces the harsh glare of justice. Or the icy soaking tub of justice. Or whatever kind of justice will hurt that lying, scheming, fellow-female-sabotaging jerk the worst.

If only I could get back into her damned emails.

Hack into them, even...

"Hack them..." I bite my lip, thoughts racing as I jab the button for the ground floor and whip out my cell.

On the way down in the elevator, I scroll through my contacts.

My college friend Gregory is not a source, but he owes me a solid—not just for bailing on drink night with me and my stupid ex, but for the strings I pulled for him with the alumni committee, guaranteeing he and his wife could get married at the Harvard Natural History museum where they met. He's also a dynamite hacker. He put most of that behind him when he graduated, but I'm pretty sure I can convince him to come out of retirement for a good cause.

If I find the evidence I need, Jack and Ryan will forgive my unorthodox methods. And if I don't, neither of them needs to know I went looking. But I have to look, not simply to finish what I started, but to protect the company and the men I love.

I do love them. Both. So much.

And I get to keep loving one of them.

Ryan will eventually forgive me. Blood is thicker than disappointment or anger. We'll make up and move on, and someday—aside from the aching chasm in my chest where Jack used to live—it will be like this never happened.

The thought should be at least a little comforting.

But it isn't. Not at all.

# CHAPTER 21

## Jack

Day 28 Tue 8/28
*One week later...*

Who knew a mustache could bring so much heartache?

Last month, if someone had told me I'd be bailing on my morning meeting to sit at my desk alone, obsessively petting a three-inch strip of fake man-fuzz and damn near crying into my coffee, I probably would've decked the guy.

And yet, here I sit.

I stole the 'stache—the original prototype she wore on her interview—from Ellie's place the last time I was there. I'd planned to use it for some over-the-top prank to make her laugh. Now it's just a sad, fuzzy reminder of what we used to have. Of all the things I let slip through my fingers.

This week has been a banner one for Seyfried & Holt. Ryan and Rictor locked in Ian Fox, his teammate Justin Cruise, and two more of their very wealthy Portland Badgers teammates. I have Walker Dunn scouting potential clients on the Buffalo Tempest. Revenues are up, the market is hot, our clients are happier than they've ever been, and Blair is on vacation.

She's sticking to her story, backpedaling slightly to account for Ellie's big gender reveal—now she's claiming Ellie must've used some kind of fake rubber cock to intimidate her.

Rubber cock.

Seriously. It was all I could do not to tell her about Ellie's tube sock.

Despite her bullshit story, Blair got legal to back off, and now she's out of my hair for a few weeks, tucked away on a tropical island sipping daiquiris while I read through employment law books and figure out a way to legally drop her ass.

Despite Blair's nonsense and the dip in morale after Ellie's undercover role came to light, it wasn't long before the team was back in good spirits, thanks in part to the changes we've started implementing—work-from-home options, flexible schedules, clearer HR policies, better on-the-job training, and more pathways for advancement. The staff are thrilled with the new benefits, and Ryan and I will end up with a healthier, more productive workforce. Everyone wins.

If Ellie showed up today to write her original article —the "Not your mother's Wall Street" one—Seyfried & Holt would pass with flying colors.

Irony, sweet irony.

Someday, I might look back on this and laugh my balls off.

But today is not that day.

Today, and yesterday, and every damn day since I last saw Ellie has brought me nothing but pain. It's like someone tossed me out the fifty-eighth-floor window then found me on the pavement and stomped on my chest, just in case my heart was still intact.

Newsflash: it isn't.

But Ellie made it clear she doesn't want anything to do with me.

So here I sit, a lonely, office-dwelling, mustache-petting weirdo, wondering if I'll ever taste that woman's sweet kiss again. If I'll ever get rid of the aching black hole in my heart, punched through in the perfect, unforgettable shape of Eleanor Seyfried.

# CHAPTER 22

## Ellie

Day 29 Weds 8/29

*I* try to stay focused on the positive—Gregory is on the case and compiling digital evidence I'm almost certain will prove my suspicions about Blair —but it's not easy. My apartment, my neighborhood, my favorite Indian restaurant where I used to enjoy a soul-nourishing meal—all of them are haunted by memories of Jack.

It's so bad that I find myself cruising Craigslist, looking at apartments and wondering if I have the will or the money to move, when an unexpected notification pings from my personal email, offering a reprieve.

To: Eleanor Seyfried
    From: Lulu Rivera

Hey, Ellie. I hope it's okay that I'm emailing you here —Jack gave me your info.

Just wanted to say thank you for talking to Jack about my situation. He called me this morning to offer me my job back. Actually, he offered me a promotion! Starting tomorrow, I'll be working with Hannah, shadowing her until I'm ready to take over her position while she moves on to train as a broker. I'm so excited I can barely contain myself, and it's all thanks to you! Well, and Eric. ;)

I know people are upset about what happened, but I understand why you did what you did. And I would love it if we could still be friends. The things I liked about Eric aren't going to change because you took off your fake mustache.

Plus, you still owe me a happy hour rendition of *Shot Through the Heart*, and I'm holding you to it! ;-) My cell number's in the signature if you ever want to chat.

Hugs and more thanks!

—Lulu

BLINKING BACK GRATEFUL TEARS, I hit the number for her cell and text: *Hey, it's Ellie! I'm so happy for you, Lulu. This news made my day, and I would be honored to be your friend. I need all the friends I can get. Especially if I have to sing in public. :-)*

After only a second or two, Lulu pings me back. *Wonderful! Me, too. Want to meet up tonight? My ex has the kids, and I'm going out for munchies and margaritas at the Mexican place on Fulton to celebrate. No karaoke, but the queso dip is out of this world.*

.  .  .

MY FIRST INSTINCT is to confess that I'm not good company right now and beg off. But that's what the old Ellie would do, and I don't want to go back to lurking in my writer lair with nothing but a block of sharp cheddar cheese to keep me company. I've had a taste of what it feels like to have a fuller, richer life, and I refuse to backslide again, no matter how down in the dumps I am.

*Sounds amazing,* I tap before I can talk myself out of it. *Though, I'll warn you, I'm a little out of sorts. The truth coming out the way it did has been rough.*

*I can imagine,* Lulu responds, *but it will all blow over. I promise. Bad things always do, and then the good stuff is still there. Good has staying power.*

I shake my head as I rise from the couch to pace the hardwood floor where Jack held me in his arms for that first dance. Lulu's optimism is impressive, especially after all she's been through with her ex and the kids. *You're an inspiring lady, Lulu. Jack picked the perfect person to take over for Hannah. I have no doubt you'll do an incredible job.*

*Thank you!* Lulu sends a smiley face and a heart before dropping something unexpected. *And he picked the perfect person to fall in love with, too. You guys are good together.*

*Um... Did he say something?* My thumbs fly as my thoughts race. Is it possible that he feels that way? Even now?

*He didn't have to. It's obvious every time he looks at you,* Lulu shoots back. *Even when you were Eric! But my suspi-*

*cions were confirmed when we met today. Every time your name
came up, he got THE LOOK. You know the look.*

I pace faster, my pulse picking up, too. I need to
know if there's a chance—even a minuscule one—that
he's missing me as much as I'm missing him. *Really? You
could tell from the way he looked at me even when I was Eric?
Seriously?*

*Yes, seriously.* She sends over an eye-rolling emoji. *So I
hope you're not thinking of doing something crazy like walking
away from him because of work drama. He's an amazing guy
and they don't grow on trees. Believe me, I've been checking
every branch.*

Biting my lip, I pause, gaze fixed on the turntable
where Sam Cooke still sits, ready to pick up where Jack
and I left off.

Maybe Lulu is right. Maybe I should listen to her,
and to the inner voice that convinced me to agree to
dinner in the first place.

Yes, jumping back on board the love train is a lot
scarier than grabbing nachos with a friend. But they're
both part of saying yes—yes to life and all the beautiful,
scary, wonderful, terrifying things that means. They're
both part of realizing that safety is overrated and that
only the brave get to love and be loved, but that the risk
is totally worth it.

There is no greater reward. Even three weeks with
Jack was enough to convince me of that beyond the
shadow of a doubt.

So why am I sitting here feeling sorry for myself
when I could be saying yes? Yes to everything. To all of
it, from friends and family to work to falling in love and
everything in between.

*See you at six, wise one?* I tap out as I step into my clogs, grab my laptop and my purse, and reach for the door. *I have a few things I need to take care of ASAP.*

Lulu's emoji fist makes me smile. *Go kick ass and take names girl! See you then.*

Thirty minutes later, I'm at the Neptune diner, perched on a stool with a view of the cars streaming down Astoria Boulevard as I start my article. It's not the article I'd planned to write, but it's the one I need to write, the one that's knocking around in my heart, demanding to be let out.

Even though it's by far one of the most terrifying things I've ever written.

When I'm done with my final draft, I call my brother and tell him why I don't regret what I did, why he shouldn't, either, and why I'm in love with Jack. Ryan's not on board at first, but I don't give up. I push forward, fighting to make him understand, until my brother's secretly romantic heart melts.

Then I tell him that he'll have to call Dad himself on Sunday nights from now on because I refuse to continue to facilitate their dysfunctional relationship, and I end the call while I'm ahead.

All that's left to do now is proof my article and send it to Denise.

So I do, even though the old Ellie voice in my head insists she'll hate it. Or worse, that she won't even respond to the submission.

Instead, come five-thirty, as I'm walking to the train to meet Lulu at Casa Diablo, a text from Denise informs me that my article will go live tomorrow morning, my payment is being processed, and my ability to take lemons and make lemonade is a goddamn inspiration.

I'm back in Denise's good graces and my confession will soon be live, out on the web for all the world to see.

But I don't care about the world.

Well, I do...

Of course, I do...

But at the moment, I care most about one man, the one I hope will read my story and see what I want him to see—a woman who wants to give love a chance because he showed her it was worth the risk.

# CHAPTER 23

## Jack

Day 30 Thu 8/30

From the moment Ryan sends me the link and Ellie's byline pops up on the screen, my heart is in my throat. It takes me a good ten minutes to read past the first line of her article, and even then I can't quite make my lungs exhale.

After more than a week of radio silence, simply seeing her name again nearly undoes me.

But curiosity wins out, and I read on.

THE BARRINGTON BEAT
**Walk Like a Man, Fall Like a Woman**
*By Eleanor Seyfried, Contributing Writer*

YOU KNOW THE OLD SAYING, never judge a man until you've walked a mile in his shoes? Here's what I'm wondering: if wearing his shoes earns you the right to judge, what do you get for walking around in a suit and a fake mustache, with your boobs mashed to your chest and a tube sock stuffed in your underwear?

I'll tell you what you get, people: an honorary membership in the boys' club.

More than you ever wanted to know about the state of the men's bathroom.

A fair bit of chafing, if we're being honest.

And, if you're really lucky, a chance at love.

These are not hypotheticals.

For three weeks, I went undercover as a dude in one of the most dude-dominated industries of the modern age: finance. I went into this assignment with a hypothesis that I intended to prove correct: that women are less likely to be hired for executive positions, that we're paid less for doing the same jobs, that we're given fewer opportunities for career advancement, that we're punished for the biological ability to bear children, and that we're much more likely than our male counterparts to be the victims of unwanted sexual advances.

Posing as a male stockbroker, I entered the work-force at a boutique investment firm, seeking to expose the seedy underbelly of the patriarchy (yes, I actually used that exact phrase) from the inside. Dressed in a suit and decked out in enough stage makeup to make die-hard theater geeks everywhere beam with pride, I stealthily interviewed employees, eavesdropped on conversations, correlated hiring and firing records, and bore witness to all sorts of systemic bias in a business environment so steeped in dude-bro culture it didn't know a maxi pad from a maxi dress.

That the finance industry is rife with discriminatory practices, gender bias, and sexual harassment will come as no surprise to any woman who's ever set one peep-toed foot on Wall Street—or worked in any job with men in positions of greater power, for that matter—and my research in that area revealed few, if any, surprises.

As expected, I found enough evidence to back up my assumptions two, four, ten times over.

You might say that my original premise wasn't all that original.

You might also say that I blew my cover, compromised my story, and hurt a lot of people along the way.

You'd be right on all counts.

And since we're all friends here, I have another confession: somewhere between the first time I glued on that sweet Tom Selleck mustache and the last time I stuffed my drawers with that less-sweet tube sock, I accidentally fell in love with the boss.

I don't mean the red-hot, heart-skipping, schoolgirl-crush-on-steroids kind of love, either—though there was certainly a lot of red-hot crushing going on. I mean the kind of love that makes you truly *believe* for the first time in your life—not just in love, or fairytales, or great golden possibilities.

The kind of love that makes you believe in *yourself*. In your strength. In your gifts and your specialness as a human being seeking a meaningful connection with another human being, despite all the obstacles, misunderstandings, and human flaws.

When you consider everything working against us,

the odds of finding your one capital-P Person feel down-right impossible, don't they? I mean, I went into this experiment assuming that most men were incapable of—or, at the very least, highly resistant to—growing emotionally, showing vulnerability, or admitting their mistakes. And my assumptions about women weren't any better. Women, I believed, were too afraid of our own power to actually do anything to take it back.

I was arrogant and stubborn and plain-old wrong in almost every possible way (except the falling in love part, but we'll get back to that).

The truth is, we're all a bunch of walking paradoxes. We are sensitive and brash, emotional and guarded, cowardly and courageous, horribly stubborn and yet capable of profound change.

It's society that tries to shove us into pink and blue boxes, to make us question the way we look, the clothes we wear, the way we speak, the way we walk, the kinds of things we're interested in. According to some fancy-pants sociologists, even the way we chew our food is a marker for gender identity!

This social compartmentalization is unnatural at the most primal, basic level, and it hurts every last one of us. At home, at work, in our families, in our friendships, in our marriages and partnerships. It hurts our children. It hurts our future. We're taught from childhood to fear what makes us different rather than embrace it, and the lingering effects of that fear are staggering. During my brief time on Wall Street, I saw up close and personal all the ways in which we allow those differences to become dividers, those dividers to become justifications, those justifications to become weapons.

It doesn't have to be this way. I believe that each of us has the power to break out of our confining boxes and refuse to be shoved back inside. And most importantly, to stop forcing our fellow humans to conform to narrow definitions that do nothing but starve all of us of light, love, connection, and collective greatness.

Wiser people than I have said that real change comes slowly, if at all. Perhaps this is true. But it's not a reason to give up. I know, I trust, and I *believe* that change is possible.

Despite all my fumbling, stumbling, and bumbling— tube sock between the legs, remember—I still managed to expose some of the core discriminatory issues at the investment firm. With guidance and support from the firm's incredible—wait, scratch that—from the firm's *badass* female staff, the leadership team has already begun implementing changes to make the company an equal, challenging, and rewarding place for *all* of its team members.

And despite all my fumbling, I still managed to experience real human connection, friendship, and yes, love.

Allow me to close with a few precious nuggets of hard-earned wisdom:

1. Assumptions might make an ass out of you and me, but if you have the opportunity to challenge them, take it. And if you don't have the opportunity, make one! This might mean an elaborate disguise, but it could also mean something as simple as talking to a new person, reading a book, wandering into a different neighborhood, or simply asking yourself if there's any room for your opin-

ions to change. (Spoiler alert: there's always room for change).

2. A tube sock between the legs, while fun at parties and an excellent conversation starter, does not a real man make. Which is to say you can never truly *become* another person, but empathy and compassion begin with putting yourself in someone else's shoes. If each of us committed to practicing that on even the smallest level —at work, or within our own group of family and friends —just think what we might accomplish together! Most importantly...

3. When you find your capital-P Person, the one who sees through your disguise and deep down to your soft, squishy, longing-for-connection heart, don't be Ellie. Don't screw it up. I know it's scary, but find your bravery. Own it. Open up your heart and let love in. And don't let that person get away.

ONE FATEFUL AFTERNOON, I put on a pair of men's shoes and started walking my mile in hopes of changing the workplace environment for a group of women swimming against the current in a sea of inequity.

But in the end, the thing that changed most profoundly was myself.

And that, my friends, is when the real journey begins.

.  .  .

—ELEANOR SEYFRIED

P.S. DEAREST J, on the chance that you're reading this, and on the chance that it isn't *completely* obvious... Even without my mustache and tube sock, I'm still madly in love with you.

\* \* \*

HALF AN HOUR LATER, I've read it more times than I can count. My head is spinning. I'm so proud of my girl, so happy to see her hard work come to fruition, even if it wasn't how either of us had planned. The story went live two hours ago, and the damn thing has already gone viral.

The question on everyone's mind—and comment thread, and Facebook and Twitter feeds—is this:

*#WWDJD?*

What will "Dearest J" do?

Well, as a man who makes his living wooing wealthy clients and convincing them to part with oodles of hard-earned cash, I'm nothing if not a goddamn *expert* in customer satisfaction.

Before the closing bell, the People of the Internet will have their answer.

And so will Ellie.

I leave a quick message for Hannah and Lulu to reschedule my meetings for the rest of the day, grab my phone, and take off with a master plan to win back the love of my life. Well, not so much a master plan as a half-cocked scheme and a fool's hope that my Capital-P

Person meant what she said in that postscript, and that she'll give me a chance to prove how madly in love I am, too.

With or without her porn 'stache.

Like all the most worthwhile endeavors, making my move is a risk. A big one. But if I've learned anything about Ellie, it's that she's a sucker for a wild scheme and a fool with a big enough tube sock to pull it off.

By the time I hit Vesey Street, I'm ready.

With a deep breath and another dose of blind hope, I pull out my phone, scroll to find the contact info I saved that day on the Great Lawn, and hit the call button.

Spencer answers on the first ring.

"Hey, it's Jack Holt," I say. "Can I ask you for a really crazy favor?"

# CHAPTER 24

## Ellie

Day 30 Thu 8/30

*W*ithin minutes of my Barrington piece going live this morning, Ryan texted me to tell me he's proud of me and wants to meet for lunch tomorrow, but hours stretch on with no word from Jack.

I clean my apartment from top to bottom, reorganize my workspace, and compile a list of new article ideas to pitch to Denise, but still my phone remains ominously silent.

It isn't until I'm about to hop in the shower to wash last night's Mexican fiesta-stink out of my hair that my cell finally buzzes. I snatch it from my desk in a rush of excitement, but the text isn't from Jack.

It's Gregory, warning me that I've got one hell of an email coming, compiling evidence that Blair and William Pool—Lulu's former asshole supervisor—have been using Blair's connection at the Department of Justice to get insider information on pending mergers, which they've been using to very illegally make themselves and a few of Will's clients very rich.

So *that's* the deal he and Blair were chatting about.

Even though I know once the Feds get involved the news will bring increased scrutiny to S&H and everyone working there, I can't help victoriously fist-pumping my way around the apartment.

I'm not usually the kind to take pleasure in another's pain, but Blair is more of a narcissistic, criminal, mean-spirited troll under the bridge of Ryan and Jack's company than a person, and Will is a greedy jerk who made Lulu cry.

I celebrate their imminent downfall by pouring myself a glass of white wine and sipping it as I page through the treasures Gregory has uncovered.

An hour later, I've finished reading the file and am composing an email to break the news to Ryan and Jack, when my cell buzzes again.

This time, the name is the one I've been waiting for, the one that makes my heart leap into my throat and stay there, pulsing with a frantic mixture of hope and anxiety.

Unfortunately, the content of Jack's message doesn't give me much to go on as far as how he's feeling about me—*Need to talk, Ellie. Can we meet for a drink at Masala?*

Swallowing hard, I text back, *Yes. Thirty minutes?*

After only a moment, he responds, *Perfect. I'll be there.*

Deciding the email to Ryan and Jack can wait— better to warn Jack in person about what's coming, hopefully after he's told me he's willing to give us another chance—I rush to the bathroom to shower. If my hopes are dashed and Jack decides to tell me goodbye forever, I don't want to smell like a burrito while it's happening.

I complete the world's fastest primping routine— washing, drying, and curling the ends of my hair before putting on enough makeup to hide how poorly I've been sleeping since all the shit hit the fan—and hurry down the hall.

I'm waiting for the elevator when Spencer's door opens and Sonia sticks her head out, a huge smile on her face.

"Heading out for a hot date?" she asks, a twinkle in her eye that makes me worry she's changed my ring tone.

"Just going to see a friend." My toes squirm in my shoes as I wonder if a white sundress, brown shawl, and cowgirl boots looks like I'm trying too hard.

I'm debating rushing back to change into jeans, when Sonia giggles. "Whatever you say." Her dimples pop. "But take pictures for me, okay?"

I frown, but before I can ask her what she's up to, the elevator door pings open and Sonia waves goodbye with a merry, "Good luck!"

Unease prickles across my bare arms, making me feel like I walked through a spider web, but I step into the elevator anyway and hit G for the ground floor. Whatever Sonia the Prank Master is up to, I don't have time to dig deeper right now.

A few minutes later, I step into Masala and scan the small bar area, where a giant blue Buddha watches over the bearded man mixing drinks for a smattering of customers. There's a couple I recognize from the neighborhood laughing it up near the fountain in the corner, but all the other patrons gathered at the bar's high tables or perched on barstools are women.

Deciding Jack must still be in transit, I cross to the bar and claim a seat at the far end, near the garnish station. I usually find the smell of orange and lemon slices soothing, but tonight I'm too on edge. I pull out my phone to check if a text from Jack might have slipped through unnoticed, when a pair of very stylish—and very large—heels appear in my peripheral vision and a voice asks, "Is this seat taken?"

I glance up, an apology for needing to keep the stool free on my lips, but the moment I see the person standing with a hand braced gracefully on the bar beside me, the words are lost. My eyes fly open wide, my jaw drops, and a strangled sound gurgles from my chest. I don't know whether to be shocked, amused, horrified, or a mixture of all three, but I know the moment I meet Jack's expertly made-up smoky-eyes that everything is going to be all right.

I don't know much about romance, but having an alpha male without a cross-dressing-curious bone in his body gear up in drag for me is absolutely the most romantic event of my life.

Bar none.

"What on earth?" I ask, my lips curving.

"I didn't want to tell you I'm on your side again, Eleanor," he says, brushing his long hair over his shoulder. "I wanted to walk my mile in your shoes and show you."

"Wow." I blink faster as my gaze skims up and down, taking in his silky brunette wig, deftly applied makeup, and figure-skimming green dress. He's wearing a stuffed bra of some kind, in addition to panty hose, and should look ridiculous. But even though he's one of the tallest "women" I've ever seen, he doesn't.

"You're a surprisingly pretty woman, Mr. Holt," I say as he settles into the seat next to mine, making my heart lift as the familiar smell of him rushes through my head.

God, I've missed his smell. Nine days without it is too much.

"Thank you." Jack sets his small clutch on the bar and reaches out to take my hand, making me grin wider even as the back of my nose begins to sting. "But I'll confess I had help. Spencer really is a genius with makeup."

I laugh, Sonia's request for a picture making sense now.

"I read your article," Jack says in a softer voice.

"Yeah?" My throat locks up and my pulse races as I realize this is it, the moment I find out if Jack feels the way I feel. Considering he's literally walked here in women's shoes—a size thirteen or fourteen satin pump to be exact—things are looking good, but there's too much at stake not to be on the edge of my seat.

I lean forward, gaze locked on his as he continues, "You weren't plain old wrong, the way you said in the article. *I* was wrong. I should have given you more time instead of letting fear call the shots."

"We all let fear call the shots sometimes. I certainly did." I take a deep breath, tongue sweeping out to dampen my lips as I confess, "I shouldn't have left the office the way I did. I should have stayed and talked it out. Or at least taken your calls after that. I was just...

overwhelmed. My feelings for you, all the stuff I was uncovering, the lies Blair told... I regressed, and I'm sorry."

"I understand." He gives my hand a gentle squeeze. "I fumbled the pass, El. I should have put myself in your shoes a week ago. I'm sorry I made you wait. Can you ever forgive me?"

I smile even as my throat goes tight. "I think that can be arranged."

"Yeah?" His glossy lips curve in that vulnerable just-for-Ellie grin that's become so precious to me. "And how about being my Capital-P Person? And letting me be yours? Because you locked down my heart the first time you swaggered out of the bathroom with a sock stuffed down your pants."

"Well, since we're doing confessions...that first time wasn't a sock. It was a shower cap stuffed with TP." I laugh, but the sound fades to a sigh as he continues, saying the words I've been dying to hear.

"I love you, Eleanor Seyfried." His green eyes seem to shine from the inside, leaving no doubt in my mind that he means every word. "You are everything I want in a partner and everything I was too stupid to realize I needed until you turned my world upside down and showed me the beautiful things I was missing. Will you be my Capital P?"

I curl my fingers around his as tears fill my eyes. But they're happy tears. Grateful tears. "Yes, Jack Holt," I say, with a sniff. "I would be honored to be your Capital P. I love you, too. So much."

"Thank God." Relief fills his eyes as he wraps his arms around me, drawing me off my stool and into a fierce hug that makes me feel so safe and precious that not even Jack's fake boobs pressing against my chest can make the moment anything less than perfect.

Then he kisses me, soft and sweet and then deeper, claiming my lips the way he's claimed my heart. I wrap my arms around him and hold on tight, grateful that I live in a neighborhood where a woman and a man dressed in drag can make out at a bar without anyone batting an eye, and even more grateful for this man, this chance, this shot at forever that I'm going to fight for with every ounce of passion I've got.

Which reminds me...

I pull away from the kiss with a deep breath. "Blair and Will have been using insider info from someone at the DOJ to run their own scheme on the side. I have evidence. I was about to send it over when you texted."

Leaving Gregory's name out of it, I give him the scoop, including the fact that Blair's shady behavior made my hackles raise, and how I couldn't ignore my intuition.

Jack's eyes narrow. "That scheming, conniving—"

"Monster jerk," I provide.

"I was going to say asshole," Jack says, "because I've learned not to use gendered words like 'bitch' that I wouldn't use if I were talking about a man. But yeah, monster jerk works. Scum is also good." He curses beneath his breath. "I can't believe she put our company at risk this way. We were good to her. Not to mention, Will. He was one of our first hires, someone we thought we could count on to put S and H first."

"They screwed up," I say, feeling terrible for him. For me, this is a win, but for him it's proof that his trust was both misplaced and abused. "But you didn't. They were sneaky, both of them. I almost missed it myself."

"But you didn't," he says. "Because you're tenacious, ferocious, and have killer instincts."

"And I had a little help in the electronic snooping department."

Jack lifts a brow. "More friends in high places?"

"Something like that. I just hope everything we've got is enough."

"I'm sure the lawyers and the feds will take it from here." Jack blows out a breath, shaking his head in disbelief. "Wow. I still feel like a fucking idiot."

"You're not." I lean in to kiss his cheek. "You're drop-dead sexy. And smart. And brave. And a knockout as a man *or* a woman, which is pretty impressive."

His lips curve. "Flattery is appreciated, but I'm still mad as hell."

I nod, watching him carefully. "But you're not mad at me, right? That I kept digging after you wanted me to stop?"

"No, I'm not. Like I said, you've got killer instincts, El. And from now on I'm going to do my best to trust them."

I link my wrists behind his neck with a grin. "Yeah?"

"Yeah." His smile goes naughty around the edges. "How about we forget the drink and head up to your place? I want to see if you're as good at getting bras off as I am."

I giggle. "I've had over a decade of practice. I'm an expert."

"Ah, but not at getting them off of *other* people." He

takes my hand, drawing me across the room. "And not while I'm doing my best to get you out of *your* bra first."

"Are we betting again? High-stakes orgasms?"

"I wouldn't have it any other way."

"Sounds like a win-win," I murmur.

"It's all winning, baby," he promises as we swing outside into the warm summer afternoon, "from here on out."

Later—as I'm laughing so hard tears stream down my face as I help Jack wrestle out of a pair of control-top pantyhose, which turn out to be far more challenging than the bra—I make a mental note to start journaling again, the way I did when I was a kid.

I don't want to forget a moment of my life with this magical man. I want to wrap every memory up with a bow and tuck it away for safekeeping.

\* \* \*

BUT AS THE MONTHS PASS, Jack and I growing closer than I've ever been to another person, I find I'm too busy living—and loving—to write everything down. I'm also too busy studying for my Series 7 and 63 exams. Turns out, I actually enjoy working in finance, especially for a company that truly *isn't* your mother's Wall Street —not since Jack and Ryan began charting a new course.

Every day brings a new, exciting challenge, stretching my mind in creative directions that I never could've predicted. Hannah, Lulu, and the rest of my karaoke ladies welcome me back with open arms, and even Rictor and I bury the hatchet. He's the first to congratulate me when I kick his ass in fantasy baseball, and even asks my advice on emerging tech before expanding his portfolio to include stocks in a smart-home startup company.

I love my new job, but I haven't given up writing.

I'm working on a memoir I sold to a major publishing house not long after my article went viral, and my new agent is pitching a how-to guide for women in the workplace. I'm also writing a romance novel. Turns out I have a lot to say about love. About how amazing and inspiring and life-changing it is.

And how my boyfriend's penis is the best penis on the entire planet.

"You can't put that in your novel," Jack says, kissing my cheek on his way into the kitchen to grab Sunday morning coffee.

"About your penis?" I cock my head, studying the line. "Why? It's factual."

"But this is for your novel, not the memoir, correct?"

"Truth lends verisimilitude to fiction." I grin at him as I wiggle my fingers toward the coffeepot. "Bring me more coffee, please?"

"Only if you take out the part about my dick."

My lips turn down in an exaggerated frown. "Don't be selfish."

"It's *my* dick," he says, plucking the pot from the warmer with a wicked grin. "And I don't think I've been the least bit selfish with it."

I sigh, skin heating as I remember how not-selfish he was with every inch of his sexy-as-hell body last night.

"I can arrange to be equally unselfish this morning." He gives the liquid in the pot a swirl. "Assuming you play your cards right."

"In that case, your dick shall remain our closely guarded secret." I highlight the last paragraph and hit delete. "The offensive sentence is gone. Meet you in bed in ten seconds?"

"Five, baby." He sets the pot down and makes a break for his bedroom, slapping me on the bottom on the way by. "Get that fine ass in gear."

I do, and his generosity is as sexy and blissful as ever.

Afterward, I bring us both fresh coffee in bed and we snuggle under the covers to make plans for Thanksgiving at my dad's place and Christmas in the Rockies and all the adventures we can't wait to have together—me and this man who is my partner, my true love, my best friend, my Nuclear Fab-Gasm giver, and everything in between.

# CHAPTER 25

## Jack

Four Months Later...

"*I*'m sorry, Jack. I didn't mean to leave you behind on the last run. I guess I just didn't realize I was built for speed."

Standing inside Breckenridge Ski and Board Rental, Ellie grins as she steps back into her regular snow boots, victory written all over her pink-cheeked face.

She's wearing a pair of blissfully tight white ski pants and a fitted jacket that hugs every curve, and when she bends over to tie her boots, I let my eyes drift to the twin snow globes of her perfect ass.

"Built for speed *and* for that outfit," I say. "Frankly, I'm glad I fell behind. I had an amazing time watching your ass swish down the slope. And feel free to stay in that position for as long as possible. Or we can head back out..."

Laughing, she stands up and turns around, admonishing me with a faux-warning glare. "Enough winter sports for one day, Holt. Take me back to the cabin and thaw me out, or you'll be stuck with a popsicle for Christmas."

"But that works out perfectly. I was just telling Santa all I really want for Christmas is to lick your—"

"Jack Edward Holt, there are *children* around!"

"You know you love me," I whisper. "Dirty jokes and all." I press a family-friendly kiss to her lips, then we hop on the shuttle back to our home away from home—a charming A-frame cabin nestled in the woods outside town, our very own winter wonderland.

Since Ellie was the conquering hero of the slopes today, I leave her to warm up in front of the fireplace with a glass of Malbec while I cook Christmas Eve dinner—and by "cook," I mean warm up the roast turkey and fixings we picked up at Whole Foods on the drive from the airport.

After we've stuffed ourselves silly, I make hot chocolate with Bailey's and we settle in on the couch to stare at the crackling flames, the perfect wind-down to another perfect day with Ellie.

Ellie...

I look at her now, curled up in yoga pants and a blue fleece at the end of the couch, her lips pursed as she blows on her hot chocolate, the fire popping, and I'm nearly overcome with gratitude. Everything I've endured in my life—the successes and failures, the hardships as well as the triumphs—it was all worth it. Because it all led me right here. To the woman I love. The woman I'm meant to honor and cherish and adore for the rest of my life.

I've never been more certain of that than right now.

"Be right back, baby." Swallowing the knot of emotion in my throat, I slide off the couch and duck out before she catches me getting misty-eyed. In the kitchen, I dig into the back of the pantry, unearthing the gift from where I so carefully hid it.

"Merry Christmas, El." Back in the living room, I present it with a flourish, loving the way she laughs in response.

"A bag of Cheetos?" She shakes her head with a grin. "Aw, baby, you shouldn't have. You're too good to me."

"Never. I'm just good enough. And it reminds me of the last Christmas we spent together, hiding out in your dad's basement."

Her gaze softens. "Me, too. But please tell me you didn't bring a joint this time."

"No, but now that you mention it..." I wriggle my eyebrows. "It's legal here. I could make a midnight run."

"No thanks, stoner boy. I'm content with Cheetos. And the good news is, I'm no longer wearing white snow pants." Ellie sits up straight on the couch, reaching for the bag and popping it open in with a well-practiced yank. "I'm going in."

She peeks into the bag, her smile melting into a confused frown.

"Is there a problem with your gift, Eleanor?" I ask.

"They're all white. No, they're..." She reaches inside and pulls out a handful of Styrofoam packing peanuts. Casting a narrow glance my way, she asks, "What are you up to, Jack Holt?"

"Looks like Santa screwed up my order. It's like I always say, El. If you want something done right, you have to do it yourself." I blow out a mock sigh of frustration then crouch on my knee in front of her, my hands sliding up her thighs. "Did he leave a note or anything?"

"Let me check." Grinning like—well, the proverbial kid on Christmas, Ellie digs deeper into the bag, retrieving a small box wrapped in shiny silver paper and tied with a silky white ribbon.

Her eyes sparkle in the firelight, wonder lighting up her pretty face. God, she's beautiful. Inside and out. Some days I still can't even believe it's real—that she picked me. That she's here, right now, smiling at me like I'm all the man she'll ever need.

There was a time in my life—not that long ago— when that thought would've sent me running for the hills, too scared of losing something so precious to let myself believe I could keep it.

But those days are over. Every moment with Ellie is a gift—one that takes up so much room in my heart there's no longer a place for fear.

"You didn't have to do this," she says softly, leaning in to wrap her slim fingers around the back of my neck. She presses her lips to mine before pulling away, her eyes glazing with emotion. "This whole trip... everything has been so perfect... I don't know how to thank you. I'm—"

"Ellie, please open the box."

"Okay, okay," she says with a sniff and a laugh as she sits back and daintily removes the bow, taking her sweet time peeling off the tape, unfolding every corner, then finally sliding out the black velvet box.

Ellie gasps, pressing a hand to her chest.

"You're already my Capital P," I say, taking the box from her hand and opening it. "Now I want you to be my Capital F."

"Fiancée," she whispers, tears gathering in her eyes as I remove the ring from the velvet insert.

"No, my Forever." I slide it over her finger and look into her beautiful blue eyes, my entire body humming with excitement and love and a rush of emotion I can't even name, but that makes my heart soar. "Eleanor Victoria Seyfried, will you marry me?"

Ellie lets out a squeak, but she doesn't hesitate, sliding off the couch and tackling me in a fierce hug. "Yes! Yes, I will marry you, Jack Edward Holt. I will be your Capital P, Capital F, Capital everything."

Fighting my own tears, I pull her into a deep, Bailey's-and-cocoa kiss, committing everything about this moment to memory. The sweet taste of her mouth, the hot brush of her fingers as she tugs my shirt over my head, the love in her eyes as I stroke her wet heat.

We don't even make it to the bedroom.

As the snow covers Breckenridge, Colorado, in a heavy white blanket, and our fire pops and crackles behind us, I make love to my fiancée, my forever, the fierce and amazing woman who marched into my office one day with a fake mustache and a hunch and walked out with my heart.

Later, after we've celebrated more times than we can count, when the fire has burned down to embers and Christmas morning dawns with a pale pink sunrise over the treetops, Ellie snuggles against my chest, her lips brushing my ear as she whispers, "But you still have the Cheetos from the bag somewhere in this cabin, right?"

Truly, I couldn't love her more.

Need more steamy, feel good romance in your life?
Check out THE PLAYBOY PRINCE!

Keep reading for a sneak peek!

## SNEAK PEEK

Enjoy this sneak peek of THE PLAYBOY PRINCE!
The entire Rugged and Royal series is out now.

### CHAPTER ONE

*Sabrina Rochat*

A woman on the verge of making several
***very dumb*** decisions in the name of love

My family is crazy.

Yes, I realize that, at some point, everyone thinks their nearest and dearest would take home honors at a Worldwide Weirdo Pageant, but in my case, it's actually true.

I run nature retreats for a living, but my real full-time job is making excuses for my family's oddball behavior.

"So, it's okay to take pictures?" The timid woman

pushes her thick glasses up her nose, visibly trembling as she shoots a worried glance down the green mountain toward the castle, where my mother apparently retreated after issuing threats to my latest campers that taking pictures would "steal what's left of the kingdom's soul."

"It's absolutely okay to take pictures." I beam my brightest smile to the assembled group of women, while mentally composing a warning to my mother to quit frightening our paying customers.

I know she enjoys regular meals and internet access as much as the rest of us, though she pretends to be a starving Bohemian who can survive on angst and poetry alone.

"I take snapshots all the time for our PicsWith-Friends page. See?" Holding up my phone, I scroll slowly through the grid of literally thousands of snapshots I've taken of the mountain in the past five years. Sunset views from the summit, shots of flower-speckled spring glens, and hundreds of close-ups of local flora and fauna —it's all there, as well as the occasional obligatory shot of the castle looking hazy and romantic in the distance.

Staying on royal land is part of the draw for Camping at Rochat, but our ancestral estate is best viewed from a distance. Technically, I live in a castle—the original medieval main hall and tower still stand—but the building has been added on to by so many generations of eccentric royals that it now resembles a surrealist portrait painted by a deranged toddler.

Up close, the castle's crazy starts to show.

Much like my family's does.

I love my parents and adore my two sisters, but it

would be so nice if at least one of them knew how to behave in polite company.

"Oh, those are really good." A taller woman with long brown-and-gray braids leans in for a closer look. "You should be a nature photographer!"

"Thank you," I say, warmed by the compliment. "My father and sister are the real artists, but..."

"Photography is a valid art form," Timid whispers, a shy smile curving her lips. "I like to crochet. Sometimes I go off the pattern and make things up as I go along."

"Wild woman," I tease with a wink.

Thankfully, the joke makes her laugh and seems to put the entire company at ease, which is a relief. The group of ten college botany teachers is my first All-American booking, and I'd love for them to take positive stories about their experience back across the ocean.

"Seriously, you have talent," Braids insists, pointing a stern finger at my screen. "Don't waste it. Like I tell my students—no one will ever see the world exactly the way you do. That's why we need new scientists and artists and all the rest. Each new pair of eyes can change the world."

Touched, I nod. "That's so true. And thank you again." I tuck my phone into the back pocket of my jeans. "If you need anything before the hike this evening, please feel free to text me. In the meantime, get settled and take as many pictures as you want. Of anything you want!"

I lift a hand and back away down the path, a twinge of regret tightening my ribs.

I'd love to learn more about photography and see plants all over the world, but I can't imagine when I'd find the time to take a class or venture more than a hundred miles from home. Someone has to hold this madhouse together.

Especially now that Lizzy is leaving.

Lizzy.

Leaving…

The thought of my older-by-four-minutes sister moving six hours away to a country accessible only by air or treacherous, winding Alpine roads is bad enough. Knowing she's being sold into marriage to an idiot to secure our family's legacy is flat-out heartbreaking.

No matter how much I love this mountain, if it were up to me, I'd sell our ancestral land, put my parents up in a condo, and free us all from the royal ties that bind and gag. But clinging to history and tradition is the only thing that gets my aging father out of bed in the morning, and my mother would die of a broken heart if she knew she'd never get to see one of her girls become a "real" princess.

Since the vote that relegated our family to ceremonial status, without taxpayer support or any power over our country's governing process, my sister's betrothal to Prince Andrew of Gallantia has been the hope my mother's clung to like a sugar addict guarding the last chocolate croissant in the bakery. She's raised Lizzy to believe that marrying Andrew is her duty and destiny, and no amount of common-sense talk from my younger sister or me has been able to change Lizzy's mind.

But we've both tried. Hard.

Especially Zan.

My younger-by-ten-minutes sister, Alexandra, is a fiercely independent businesswoman presently living in

Zurich who considers arranged marriage so horrifically medieval that she plans to wear black to the wedding in protest.

Maybe it's the fact that we're triplets that's made Lizzy's fate so hard to stomach. Zan and I know that if the stars had aligned a little differently on that cold December day, it would have been one of us led to the slaughter instead of sweet, shy Lizzy.

But as Lizzy's identical twin—Zan shared a womb with us, but she doesn't share our matching DNA—I can't help but feel it's worse for me. I can sense Lizzy's emotions, even when miles separate us. I know she's miserable to be leaving home.

As I head down the trail, leaving my campers to get settled in their yurts before the guided hike this evening, I catch waves of Lizzy-flavored melancholy wafting up the mountain toward me.

Tomorrow.

Tomorrow, I will lose my sister forever.

Every time I think about it, tears prick my eyes. I've always been a look-on-the-bright-side kind of person, but lately, the sunny side has been hard to find.

I can't bear the thought of my sister married to Andrew the Atrocious.

I only spent one summer with Andrew and his brothers, but that month by Lake Lucerne was enough to make me loathe the Royal Turd. Even under the supervision of the nannies hired to watch over the six of us while our parents and the boys' grandfather drank too much German wine and debated the terms of Andrew and Lizzy's betrothal, Andrew managed to make Lizzy cry no less than ten times.

He thought his pranks—everything from the relatively benign "crickets in the oatmeal" trick to the more brutal stashing of snakes in Lizzy's bed—were hysterical. Zan and I were not amused, of course, but poor Lizzy was traumatized.

She still checks her sheets at least twice before she turns out the light, just to make sure nothing slithery is hiding under the covers.

And no, it doesn't matter that the snakes weren't venomous, or that Andrew was only nine years old. My sisters and I had only been five at the time, and all three of us knew better than to torment other children, and our parents were far more checked out of the parenting process than the Gallantian elders.

Surely, Prince Andrew had been warned by his grandfather to be kind to his future bride and her sisters, but he made a different choice. Sometimes people just turn out rotten, no matter how hard their parents and grandparents try to raise them to be decent human beings.

These days, Prince Andrew seems to be your average playboy prince, rambling around the globe with his brothers, drinking too much, partying too hard, and taking scandalous pictures with half-naked women. But I wouldn't be surprised to learn he's still got a mean streak.

Once a snake-hider, always a snake-hider.

And once they're hitched, he's going to be hiding his snake in my sister.

The thought makes my stomach turn. Lizzy deserves better. She deserves a man who worships her, a man she can't wait to share her life and her bed with.

*Which is why you have to do something, Sabrina. Now! Before it's too late.*

"But what?" I grumble as I head through the garden and into the afternoon shadows cast by the only home I've ever known. I talk a tough game, but I've never lived anywhere but here, with my parents. I was home-schooled by various nannies, got my botany degree online, and have lived a very sheltered life. I'm unfit to lock horns with a worldly opponent like Prince Andrew.

Or even my parents.

My parents mean well, but they're from another age. They were raised to believe that children should be seen and not heard, that food magically appears at the table without any effort on their part, and that the cash to fund castle expansion and a lavish ball (or four) every year is their birthright.

By the time the royal bank account finally ran dry, my sisters and I were old enough to get part-time jobs to lessen the blow, but my parents have never fully recovered from the shock of learning that the heat would have to be turned off in the west wing for the winter and that there was no money for Brie, just cheddar, the cheap kind that can be bought in bulk.

The transition was especially hard on my father, a mild-mannered but largely oblivious man who was dressed by his valet until he was in his fifties and literally had to learn how to *put on his own pants* as a full-grown man. But he still awakens every morning and dresses in a three-piece suit from his vast collection, determined to keep the glamour of the old world alive.

He will never be an ally in the fight to keep Lizzy at home, no matter how much he enjoys having someone to talk art theory with at dinner. My father thinks this marriage is a good thing.

And maybe it is. Maybe my mother's right and my mind has been warped by too much modern entertainment. Maybe love is a stupid reason to get married.

It certainly wouldn't have worked out in my case. Thor, my first and only love, adored me, but only until an heiress with a bigger bank account (and boobs) entered the picture.

I often find myself wondering if it was the boobs or the money that sealed the deal, but it doesn't really matter. Thor is gone; I don't plan on taking surgical action to alter the flatness of my chest, and my bank account is perpetually overdrawn.

Living in an ancient castle that's constantly in need of repair will do that to a girl.

As I mount the crumbling marble steps of the back veranda, I find my suited father at his easel, painting the sweeping Alpine view and the quaint village nestled in the valley below for the hundredth time.

"That's lovely, Papa." I pause to kiss his cheek and accept the usual pat on the head.

"Thank you, darling. And how are our guests? Settling in nicely?"

Initially, Papa resisted the idea of opening the estate for tourism, but framing the visitors as guests enjoying our royal hospitality won him over. That, and the steady income.

"They are. We're hosting a group of American botanists this week. They're looking forward to studying the early summer ferns."

"The ferns are delightful," Papa says, his gaze drifting back to the view. "I should paint them soon."

"I'll pick some for you on the hike this evening," I promise, kissing his cheek again, comforted by the familiar scent of oil paint and turpentine clinging to his clothes. I pull in another deep breath, savoring the smell as I step through the open door into the Great Hall and make my way up the stairs to my sister's tower studio.

He might be a little checked out, but Papa is always Papa, and there's something comforting about that. If he's excited about the royal wedding later this summer or sad that Lizzy will be leaving us, he hasn't shown it.

Lizzy's putting on a brave face, too—modeling her dresses for the engagement festivities for the family and helping Mother select gifts for her future mother-in-law —but I know better. I can feel her misery, a dark churning cloud that gets thicker and gloomier with every step I take.

By the time I mount the final stair, the sadness is oppressive.

So I'm not really surprised when I enter the room to find Lizzy lying spread eagle on the floor in the center of a circle of partially dressed mannequins with tears streaming down her cheeks.

"Oh, honey," I say, my heart in my throat. "Just call it off. You don't have to do this. You should only get married when you desperately *want* to be married, not to keep a promise made by your parents when you were too little to understand what it meant."

"It's not that." Lizzy sniffs and drags a limp arm across her damp face. "It's the collection. There's no way

I'm going to be able to finish by tomorrow. Not even if I work nonstop without eating or sleeping or peeing."

"You do pee a lot," I say, trying to lighten the mood.

I pad deeper into the room, seeking a piece of furniture that isn't covered in fabric or likely to be hiding a pin that will stick me in tender places when I sit down. My sister is a talented lingerie designer, but she's also a messy artist who thrives in chaos and believes bloody pins help make the magic happen.

"It's because I drink a lot of tea," Lizzy says, her voice quivering. "But don't make fun of me, Bree. Not now."

"I'm not making fun, I promise. Just teasing."

"Don't tease. Help me," she begs, before adding in a warning tone, "Don't sit there. I spilled soup on the cushion at lunch."

I abort my mission with a grunt, managing to reverse the bend of my knees seconds before my bottom hits the chair. "You should eat something other than soup."

"I'm too busy for anything but soup."

"You're too skinny. You need more protein in your diet."

"This isn't helping, either." She rolls her head my way, the rest of her body remaining limp on the floor. "I have to finish, Bree. I'm so close to landing a collection contract. I can feel it in my bones."

I prop my hands on my hips and survey the room. "Well, it won't be easy, but if we start now, we should be able to get everything packed and ready to ship tomorrow. Surely, they have a spare room in the castle for you to use as a studio. I mean, it's going to be your home in a month, so—"

"And when will I have time to work?" Lizzy cuts in. "I'm booked solid with engagement obligations, and I'm sure Andrew will want to spend time together before the wedding."

"He hasn't bothered in the past twenty years. Why start now?" I mutter, not bothering to keep the disdain from my voice.

Lizzy knows how I feel about her fiancé's lack of interest in her life aside from his obligatory monthly phone call and form thank-you note each year in acknowledgment of her thoughtfully crafted Christmas present.

"Because his mother will be there to make sure of it," Lizzy replies. "And I do my best work in isolation, Bree. You know that. So there's only one possible solution."

"And that is?"

"You take my place," Lizzy says, making me snort.

"Yeah, right."

"I'm serious," she whispers.

I snap my head her way, eyes going wide as I realize that she is, indeed, serious.

Dead serious.

Grab THE PLAYBOY PRINCE
wherever you like to read!

# ABOUT THE AUTHORS

Author of over forty novels, *USA Today* Bestseller **Lili Valente** writes everything from steamy suspense to laugh-out-loud romantic comedies. A die-hard romantic, she can't resist a story where love wins big. Because love should always win. She lives in Vermont with her two big-hearted boy children and a dog named Pippa Jane.

*Find Lili at...*
www.lilivalente.com

Sylvia Pierce writes steamy hockey romance and more! Visit her online at https://www.sylviapiercebooks.com

# ALSO BY LILI VALENTE

### The V-Card Diaries

*Scored*

*Screwed*

*Seduced*

*Sparked*

*Scooped*

### Hot Royal Romance

*The Playboy Prince*

*The Grumpy Prince*

*The Bossy Prince*

### Laugh-out-Loud Rocker Rom Coms

*The Bangover*

*Bang Theory*

*Banging The Enemy*

*The Rock Star's Baby Bargain*

### The Bliss River Small Town Series

*Falling for the Fling*

*Falling for the Ex*

*Falling for the Bad Boy*

### The Hunter Brothers

*The Baby Maker*

*The Troublemaker*

*The Heartbreaker*

*The Panty Melter*

## Bad Motherpuckers Series

*Hot as Puck*

*Sexy Motherpucker*

*Puck-Aholic*

*Puck me Baby*

*Pucked Up Love*

*Puck Buddies*

## Big O Dating Specialists
## Romantic Comedies

*Hot Revenge for Hire*

*Hot Knight for Hire*

*Hot Mess for Hire*

*Hot Ghosthunter for Hire*

## The Lonesome Point Series

(Sexy Cowboys)

*Leather and Lace*

*Saddles and Sin*

*Diamonds and Dust*

*12 Dates of Christmas*

*Glitter and Grit*

*Sunny with a Chance of True Love*

*Chaps and Chance*

*Ropes and Revenge*

*8 Second Angel*

## The Good Love Series

(co-written with Lauren Blakely)

The V Card

Good with His Hands

Good to be Bad

Click here to learn more

## The Happy Cat Series

(co-written with Pippa Grant)

*Hosed*

*Hammered*

*Hitched*

*Humbugged*